It's Not the End of the World

Judy Blume spent her childhood in Elizabeth, New Jersey, making up stories inside her head. She has spent her adult years in many places, doing the same thing, only now she writes her stories down on paper. More than 82 million copies of her books have been sold, in thirty-two languages. Her twenty-eight books have won many awards, including the National Book Foundation's Medal for Distinguished Contribution to American Literature.

Judy lives in Key West, Florida, and New York City with her husband. She loves her readers and is happy to hear from them. You can visit her at JudyBlume.com, follow @JudyBlume on Twitter or join her at Judy Blume on Facebook.

Books by Judy Blume

Blubber
Iggie's House
Starring Sally J. Freedman as Herself
Are You There, God? It's Me, Margaret
It's Not the End of the World
Then Again, Maybe I Won't
Deenie
Just as Long as We're Together
Here's to You, Rachel Robinson

For older readers

Forever
Tiger Eyes
Letters to Judy: What Kids Wish They Could Tell You

For younger readers

The One in the Middle Is the Green Kangaroo
Freckle Juice

The Fudge books
Tales of a Fourth Grade Nothing
Otherwise Known as Sheila the Great
Superfudge
Fudge-a-Mania
Double Fudge

The Pain and the Great One series
On Wheels!
Go Places!

It's Not
the End of
the World

JUDY
BLUME

MACMILLAN CHILDREN'S BOOKS
in association with Heinemann

First published in the US 1972 by Bradbury Press Inc.
First published in the UK 1979 by Pan Books Ltd

This edition published 2016 by Macmillan Children's Books
an imprint of Pan Macmillan
20 New Wharf Road, London N1 9RR
Associated companies throughout the world
www.panmacmillan.com

ISBN 978-1-5098-0627-0

1 3 5 7 9 8 6 4 2

A CIP catalogue record for this book is available from
the British Library.

Printed and bound by CPI Group (UK) Ltd, Croydon CR0 4YY

For John
Who married a monkey-face-maker

Chapter 1

I don't think I'll ever get married. Why should I? All it does is make you miserable. Just look at Mrs Singer. Last year she was Miss Pace and everybody loved her. I said I'd absolutely die if I didn't get her for sixth grade. But I did – and what happened? She got married over the summer and now she's a witch!

Then there are my parents. They're always fighting. My father was late for dinner tonight and when he got home we were already at the table. Daddy said hello to me and Jeff. Then he turned to Mom. 'Couldn't you have waited?' he asked her. 'You knew I was coming home for dinner.'

'Why didn't you call to say you'd be late?' Mom asked.

'It's only twenty after six. I got hung up in traffic.'

'How was I supposed to know that?' Mom asked.

'Never mind!' My father sat down and helped himself to a slice of meat loaf and some Spanish rice. He took a few mouthfuls before he said, 'This rice is cold.'

'It was hot at six o'clock,' Mom told him.

Me and Jeff kept on eating without saying a

word. You could feel what was going on between my parents. I wasn't hungry any more.

Then Daddy asked, 'Where's Amy?'

'In the den,' Mom said.

'Did she eat?'

Mom didn't answer.

'I said did she eat her supper?'

'Of course she did,' Mom snapped. 'What do you think I do – starve her when you're not around?'

My father pushed his plate away and called, 'Amy . . . Amy . . .'

Amy is six. When she doesn't like what we're having for dinner she eats a bowl of cereal instead. Then she races into the den to see her favourite TV show. But when Daddy called her she ran back to the kitchen. She gave him a kiss and said, 'Hi, Daddy.'

'How's my girl?'

'Fine.'

'Sit down at the table and drink your milk,' he said.

'First a riddle,' Amy told him.

'Okay, but just one.'

Amy is driving us crazy with her riddles. Ever since she started first grade it's been one riddle after another. And you can't tell her you already know the answer because she doesn't care. She'll keep asking anyway.

'Why did the man put Band-Aids in his refrigerator?' Amy asked.

'I give up,' my father said.

'Because it had cold cuts!' Amy laughed at her joke. She was the only one who did. 'You get it now? *Cold cuts*. The refrigerator had cold cuts! Like bologna . . . get it?'

'I get it,' Daddy said. 'That's a very good riddle. Now sit down and drink your milk.'

As Amy sat down she accidentally shook the table and her milk spilled all over the place. Mom jumped up to get the sponge.

'Don't be mad, Mommy. It was an accident,' Amy said.

'Who's mad?' my mother shouted. She mopped up the mess. Then she threw the sponge across the kitchen. It landed on the counter, next to the sink. 'Who's mad?' she hollered again as she ran out of the room and down the hall. I heard a door slam.

My mother's temper is getting worse. Last week she baked a cake. When she served it my father said, 'That's not mocha icing, is it?' And my mother told him, 'Yes, it is.' So Daddy said, 'You know I can't stand mocha. Why didn't you make chocolate?' And Mom said, 'Because I'm sick of chocolate, that's why!'

I love dessert and by then my mouth was really watering. I wished they would hurry and finish talking about it so I could start eating.

But my father said, 'I'll have to scrape off the icing.'

Mom looked right at Daddy and told him, 'Don't do me any favours!' Then she picked up that beautiful cake, held it high over her head and dropped it. It smashed at my father's feet. The plate broke into a million pieces and the chips flew all around. It was one of our ordinary kitchen plates. I'll bet if it was an antique, my mother never would have dropped it like that.

Later, when nobody was looking, I snitched a piece of cake off the floor. Even though it had fallen apart it was still delicious.

But that was last week. Tonight Mom didn't throw anything but the sponge. As she ran out of the kitchen my father cursed, crumpled up his napkin and got up from the table. Jeff pushed his chair away too, but my father hollered, 'You stay right where you are and finish your dinner!' He grabbed his coat and went out the back door. In a minute I heard the garage door open and the car start.

'You really picked a great time to dump your milk,' Jeff told Amy. He is fourteen and sometimes very moody.

'I didn't do it on purpose,' Amy said. 'You know it was an accident.'

'Well, I hope you're happy,' he told her. 'Because

the whole rotten night's ruined for all of us now!'
He cursed like my father and Amy started to cry.

'I'm going to my room,' she told us. 'Nobody
loves me any more!'

Jeff was the next one to walk out of the kitchen,
leaving me there alone. I knew where he was
going. To his private hideaway. It's on the third
floor and it used to be the spare room. The ceiling
is low on one side and the windows are small and
up high. I don't see why anybody would want to
sleep in there if he didn't have to.

Jeff spent a lot of time decorating it. There's a
big sign on the door that says *Jeff's Hideaway/All
Who Enter Do So at Their Own Risk*. Then there's a
purple light hanging from the ceiling and a million
posters all over the walls. It's very messy too. In
the fall we had to have the exterminator because
of Jeff. He took so many cookies and crackers and
cans of soda up there we got bugs. My father was
really sore! Jeff doesn't throw his garbage under
the bed any more. And he's not supposed to drink
soda anyway. It's bad for his zits. My mother calls
them pimples and says he's lucky that he's only got
one or two.

His zits don't stop the girls from calling though.
They call all the time. My father has threatened to
limit Jeff's phone conversations to two minutes.
Jeff doesn't care. There's only one girl he wants to
talk to anyway. That's Mary Louise Rumberger.

She's in his formroom. I've only seen her once. She has very nice hair and she smells like Noxzema.

I know what Jeff does up in his room. He lifts weights. Isn't that the dumbest thing? He wants to be on the wrestling team next year. My mother's worried sick because she's afraid he'll get hurt. I wonder if maybe Mary Louise Rumberger likes big muscles?

Chapter 2

The house was very quiet. I was still sitting at the dinner table, making little designs on my plate with the Spanish rice. I thought about clearing away the dishes and even stacking them in the dishwasher. But why should I? I didn't start the fight. It wasn't my fault dinner was ruined. I wondered if my mother had something special planned for dessert. I wasn't about to ask her though. She was probably locked up in her bathroom.

I went to the pantry and took down a box of chocolate-chip cookies. On my way upstairs I scooped up Mew, who was sitting on her favourite chair in the living room.

She is supposed to be the family cat but she loves me best. Probably because she knows I love *her* more than anything in the world. From far away it looks as if Mew's coat is dark grey, but when you get up close you can see that she's really striped – black, grey, a tiny bit of white and even some red here and there. She is also very fat. She wears a collar with bells around her neck. This helps do two things: One is, it warns the birds, which Mew loves to chase. And two is, it keeps her from sneaking up on you. She's very good at sneaking around. Sometimes she hides under our beds and when we walk by she jumps out. That's just her way of playing. Neither my mother nor my father is crazy about Mew and her games.

When I got to my room I closed the door with my foot and put Mew down on my bed. I flopped next to her and she stretched out. She likes me to scratch her belly. I ate my cookies and let Mew lick up the crumbs. She has never put out her claws at me. And she doesn't rip up the furniture like other cats do. It's a good thing too, because if she did we wouldn't be able to keep her.

Some people might think Mew is a dumb name for a cat. But when she came to our door two years ago she was just tiny kitten. She called *mew mew mew* and I gave her a dish of milk. She's been ours ever since. At first we all tried to think up clever names for her. But while we were thinking we got used to calling her Mew. So finally we gave up and agreed that would be her name forever.

She curled up and went to sleep as I sat down at my desk. My desk is very special. It used to be a part of somebody's dining-room set. Mom bought it for five dollars and refinished it herself. She's very good at that. Now it's bright yellow and has small gold handles on every drawer. My friends think it's neat.

I opened my middle drawer and took out my Day Book. My father gets one in the mail every December and he gives it to me. It has a plain black cover with gold letters that say *Global Insurance Company*. Inside there's a half page for every day in the year. It's not really a diary because it has no lock. It's more of an appointment book, but I don't keep a record of my appointments. If I have to go to the dentist or something like that my mother marks it on her calendar. I'm not interested in writing down that stuff.

I do keep a bunch of rubber bands wrapped around my Day Book just in case anyone happens to be snooping in my desk. They are arranged in a special way that only I understand. I took off all six of them and opened to Thursday, 25 February. At the top of the page I wrote: *Fight – E.N.'s fault*.

E.N. are my mother's initials. They stand for Ellie Newman. Her real name is Eleanor but nobody ever calls her that. My real name is Karen and nobody ever calls me anything else. It's hard to make a nickname out of Karen.

I try to be very fair about my parents' fights. Tonight was definitely my mother's fault. She should have been nicer to Daddy when he came home. She knows he likes to relax with a drink before dinner. And she shouldn't have hollered when Amy spilled her milk. That can happen to anyone.

The time Mom dropped the cake on the floor was my father's fault. He started that one by saying he hates mocha icing. So that night I wrote: *Fight*

– *B.N.'s fault.* My father's name is Bill – well, really William, but that's beside the point.

I put my pencil in my mouth and chewed on it for a while. When I was in first grade we had a contest to see who had the fewest teeth marks on his pencils at the end of the year. I lost. Biting on a pencil helps me think better.

I flipped back through the pages of my Day Book. I always give each day a mark, like on a report card. Practically every day this month has got a C.

My last A+ day was 14 December. That was a really perfect one. First of all, Gary Owens, who is a boy in my class, chose me as his partner in a spelling bee. I hope it wasn't just because I am a good speller. And second of all, Mrs Singer acted practically human. She didn't yell once. But the best thing about that day was the snow. We usually don't get that much snow so early in the season. It started in the morning and didn't stop until dinnertime. As soon as we finished eating, my father and Jeff went outside to shovel the walk. Me and Amy were dying to go out too. Finally Mom said, 'Okay . . . if you bundle up good and promise to come inside when you get cold.'

I helped Amy get ready. She has trouble with her boots. I tied up her hood and found her a pair of mittens. Then we went out together.

When Jeff saw us he called, 'How about a snow-ball fight? Me and Amy against Karen and Dad.'

'Okay,' we called.

Daddy and I hurried around to the side of our house and I made the snowballs for him to throw. Jeff and Amy hid behind the big tree and pretty soon the snow was flying. I think Daddy and I won but it didn't matter because it was such fun. When we got tired of throwing snowballs Amy and me lay down in the snow and made angels. I was moving my arms back and forth to make really good wings. Then I looked up at the sky. There were a million stars. I wanted everything to stay just the way it was – still and beautiful.

When we got up we were both soaked and I was sure Mom would yell at us. But we ran inside and she just laughed and told us we looked like snowmen. After we got into our pyjamas Mom made us hot chocolate with little balls of whipped cream on top. As I drank it I thought, I have never felt so good. Absolutely never!

Later I went up to my room and marked my Day Book A+. I didn't have to chew on my pencil to think it over. 14 December was perfect in every way.

But things have been going downhill since then. I'll bet my father will sleep in the den tonight. He's been doing that more and more. He tells us it's because my mother sits up in bed half the night watching the late show. But my mother says she can't get to sleep because Daddy snores so loud.

I marked Thursday, 25 February C−. Then I put the rubber bands back on my Day Book and went into the bathroom to brush my teeth. Maybe tomorrow will be an A+ day. I hope so.

*

Chapter 3

Debbie Bartell has been my best friend since kindergarten. She lives two blocks away. We've only been separated twice in school – in second grade and fifth. This year we're both blessed with Mrs Singer. Debbie has a younger brother the same age as Amy, so we really have a lot in common.

The trouble with Debbie is, she takes a million lessons. I only take piano, on Thursdays. But Debbie is busy five days a week plus Saturday mornings. I know her whole schedule. On Monday she's got piano. On Tuesday it's ballet. On Wednesday, Girl Scouts – on Thursday, ice-skating – on Friday, allergy shots – and art every Saturday morning.

It's all her mother's idea. Mrs Bartell wants her to try out everything. Thank goodness we're Girl Scouts together or I'd never see Debbie after school. I happen to know that Debbie wishes she had more free time to fool around and do nothing, but she doesn't want to hurt her mother's feelings. Now Mrs Bartell has found out the indoor tennis club is giving lessons to kids every Sunday afternoon. Guess what Debbie got for Christmas? A tennis racket!

★

When I met her at the bus stop this morning Debbie said, 'I don't need my allergy shots today.'

'How come?' I asked. 'It's Friday.'

'My doctor's on vacation. If I start to wheeze my mother's supposed to call some other doctor.'

'Great!' I said. 'What do you want to do after school?'

'I guess I'll come over to your house. Do you think Jeff will be home?'

'No. He's never home on Fridays. You know that. He goes to the Y to swim.'

'Oh,' Debbie said. 'I forgot. Well then . . . we might as well go to the library and get the books for our project.'

Am I wrong to feel that lately Debbie is more interested in my brother than in me? Jeff can't stand her anyway. He calls her Fat-and-Ugly right to her face. She acts like that's some kind of compliment. Maybe because she knows she's not fat *or* ugly. The truth is, she's pretty. I think Gary Owens likes her. He's always tugging at her hair. I wish he'd do that to me!

Our bus came along then and we piled in. Debbie and I always sit in the same seats – the last row on the left. We've been sitting there since I can remember. It's a twenty-minute ride to school, counting the three other stops. This morning Debbie did her maths homework on the way.

I do pretty good in school. I am also supposed to be mature, well adjusted and eager to learn. I saw this written on my permanent record card one day in the fall. Sometimes I don't feel mature, well-adjusted and eager to learn. In fact, I think my fifth-grade teacher may have mixed me up with somebody else when she wrote that.

As soon as we got to school Mrs Singer collected our milk money. I didn't know I'd forgotten mine until then. We eat lunch right in our classrooms because there isn't any cafeteria. If you don't bring your milk money on Friday you don't get any milk the following week. Sometimes, if you forget, your teacher will pay for you and you can pay her back on Monday. Mrs Singer doesn't do that. She says it is our responsibility to remember and if we don't, we have to suffer the consequences.

If Mrs Singer hadn't got married I'm sure she would still be nice. Last year whenever I went into her room with a message she was always smiling. But this year, on the very first day of school, she screamed at me in front of the whole class – just because I didn't hear her say we should open our maths books. Is that a reason to scream at a person, even if I wasn't paying attention? I was just excited because it was the first day of school. Couldn't Mrs Singer see that?

This is the first time I have ever forgotten my

milk money. Now I will have to bring something from home to drink next week. Warm juice . . . ugh! I could already tell that this was not going to be an A+ day.

Chapter 4

My father didn't come home for dinner tonight. But that's not unusual. The store is open until nine on Fridays. It's called Newman's Modern Furniture and it's out on the highway. Nothing in our house comes from the store though. That's because my mother loves old stuff. She is an antique nut. Little china babies sleep on every table in our living room. We even have an old potbellied stove, which Mom painted blue. It stands in our front hall and holds fake geraniums.

When Amy asked, 'Where's Daddy?' my mother said, 'Working late.'

On Saturday mornings my father leaves very early, same as during the week, but the rest of us sleep late. He doesn't need an alarm clock to wake him. He gets up automatically. My mother is just the opposite.

It wasn't until Saturday night at about six that I began to wonder what was going on. My parents go out every single Saturday night, rain or shine, all year long. Sometimes they argue before they go – about what they're going to do or who they're going to see – but still they go out together. The only time they stay home is if one of us is really sick.

'What time is Mrs Hedley coming tonight?' I asked, stuffing my second cupcake into my mouth.

'Don't talk with food in your mouth,' Amy said.

'Oh, shut up,' I told her. 'What time, Mom?'

Mrs Hedley has been baby-sitting since I was born. Jeff is getting pretty mad about having her come every week. He thinks he's old enough to stay alone. But my mother says if we stop using Mrs Hedley some other family will grab her.

So Jeff complains but Mrs Hedley still comes. She smells like gingersnaps. I used to like her a lot when I was little. Now I am not too crazy for her. For one thing, I am sick of holding my arms out with her knitting wool stretched across them. She spends Saturday nights making wool balls that must last her the rest of the week.

My mother sat at her kitchen desk reading the newspaper while the three of us had our supper. 'Mrs Hedley's not coming,' she said.

'She's not?'

'No.' Mom kept the newspaper in front of her face.

'How come?' I asked.

'We're not going out tonight.'

'You're not?'

'That's right.'

'How come?'

'We're just not, Karen.'

18

'Goody,' Amy said. 'Then we can all watch TV together.'

My mother put the paper down and got up to clear away the dishes. 'You can watch whatever you want. I just don't feel like any TV tonight.'

'Are you sick?' I asked.

'No.'

'Then what?'

'It's just that . . . well . . .' Mom stopped talking and looked at us. Then she shook her head and reached for a tissue. 'I'll be upstairs,' she practically whispered.

Amy finished her milk and followed my mother. Jeff took an apple out of the refrigerator, polished it on his shirt and went upstairs too.

I put the dishes in the dishwasher, then marched up to Jeff's room. I knocked. I'm not allowed in without his permission.

'What?' he called.

I had to shout because his record player was on full blast. 'It's me.'

'What?'

'I want to come in.'

'Just a minute,' he yelled. He switched off the music and opened the door.

'I'm scared,' I told him.

'Of what?'

'I don't know. I think something's wrong between Daddy and Mom.'

19

'Well, it took you long enough to figure that out.'

'I mean *really* wrong, Jeff.'

'Yeah . . . so do I.'

'Do you know anything for sure?' I asked.

'I know Dad didn't come home to sleep last night,' Jeff said.

'He didn't?'

'Nope. And I don't think he's coming back either.'

'How can you say that?'

'I can tell by the way Mom's acting. Didn't you hear her at supper? She could hardly get the words out.'

'But that doesn't mean Daddy isn't coming back.'

Jeff shrugged and walked over to his record player. He turned it on and opened a book. He was through talking to me. 'I don't believe you!' I told him. 'You don't know anything!'

Jeff didn't answer. He didn't even look up.

I went to my room and took out my Day Book. I marked Saturday, 27 February D−. I wish something would happen to make my mother and father happy again. On TV everything always turns out all right. Once I saw a show where the parents were separated. Then their little boy was kidnapped and they got together to help the FBI find him. And naturally, when they did, the kid was fine. The mother and father were so glad to see him they decided to make up and everyone lived happily ever after. It was a very nice show.

I'm sure if one of us got kidnapped my mother and father would forget about their fights and everything would work out fine. I think it would be best if Amy was the one, since she's the youngest. And everybody says she's Daddy's favourite. But who'd want to kidnap her? She's such a funny-looking kid, with big rabbit teeth and snarly hair. She is supposed to have inherited her rabbit teeth from Aunt Ruth. My mother says she'll look a lot better after she has had braces. Jeff is the good-looking one. He has a dimple in his chin and his eyes are very blue. Aunt Ruth says it's a shame to waste that face on a boy!

I am in between Amy and Jeff in looks. If I had to describe myself I would say Karen Newman is ordinary looking. I plan to do something about that in a few years. I might wear purple eyeshadow.

My father is always home on Sundays. But I checked the garage early this morning and his car wasn't there. At first I thought, maybe he's been in an accident and he's in the hospital. Maybe he's even dead! Just thinking about it made me feel sick. But he couldn't be dead. My mother would have told us. You can't keep something like that a secret.

So I went into the kitchen and mixed the pancake batter. I do that every Sunday morning. I love to crack the egg into the blender, then watch the tornado inside. Even the time I dropped the eggshell in by mistake Daddy said the pancakes were good. A little crunchy maybe, but very tasty.

We eat Sunday breakfast at ten, but at quarter after there was only me and Jeff and Amy in the kitchen. Maybe the car is at the gas station for a check-up, I thought. And Daddy is upstairs with Mom. He took a taxi home late last night and I didn't hear him come in because I was sound asleep. So naturally he and Mom are staying in bed a little later this morning. They probably were up half the night talking things over. Daddy will have his arm around Mom's shoulder when they come down for breakfast and he'll tell us we're all going into New York for the day.

'Where's Mommy?' Amy asked then.

'Still asleep,' I said.

'Where's Daddy?'

'Stop asking so many questions!' I shouted.

'The one who asks the most questions learns the most,' Amy said.

'Well today you can just learn to keep your big mouth shut!' I told her. Why did she have to interrupt just when I was planning a perfect A+ day?

I could tell Amy was going to cry. She doesn't

come right out and do it like other kids. She thinks about it for a while. You can see her face scrunch up before the tears start rolling.

Jeff dug into the Sunday papers and came up with the funnies. I threw a few drops of water on the griddle to make sure it was hot enough. When they sizzle it's ready for cooking. 'Why don't you put out the syrup, Amy?' I said. 'Your pancakes will be ready in a minute.'

'You're mad,' Amy said, sniffling.

'No I'm not.'

'You yelled at me.'

'I didn't mean to. Honest.'

'Well . . . okay then. I'll put out the syrup.' She walked over to the pantry. 'Karen . . .'

'What?'

'Do you know why the boy put his father in the refrigerator?'

'Yes.'

'Jeff . . . do you?'

'Yeah,' Jeff mumbled.

'Because he wanted cold pop! Get it?' Amy asked. '*Cold pop*, like soda.'

'That's a good riddle,' I said.

'But you already heard it . . . right?'

'Right.' I poured the batter on to the grill. I shaped it like a Mickey Mouse head. Amy loves it when I make her fancy pancakes. I shouldn't have hollered at her. After all, what does she know?

23

As soon as I gave Amy and Jeff their pancakes my mother came into the kitchen. 'Good morning,' she said. Her eyes were red and swollen.

'Look what Karen made me,' Amy said, holding up her Mickey Mouse pancake.

Mom said, 'That's beautiful. Be sure to finish it.'

Amy cut off one Mickey Mouse ear, dipped it into the syrup and ate it. 'Where's Daddy?' she asked.

Jeff looked up from his funnies. I think he was just pretending to read them anyway because he didn't laugh once.

'Daddy's busy,' Mom said.

'Doing what?' I asked.

'He's got some things to take care of. Look, you kids finish your breakfast while I go up and get dressed. Aunt Ruth will be over soon.'

She was gone before I had a chance to ask exactly what things Daddy was so busy doing.

I am so afraid Jeff is right!

Chapter 5

Aunt Ruth is my mother's older sister. She is also my mother's only living relative besides us, unless you count Mark, my cousin. But we never see him any more. He lives in Atlanta. My mother is ten years younger than Aunt Ruth and if you ask me Aunt Ruth enjoys acting like her mother. She is married to Uncle Dan, who is six feet five inches tall. When I was little he would hold me up to touch the ceiling and I thought that was really exciting. Aunt Ruth and Uncle Dan live in Maplewood. It takes about ten minutes to get from their house to ours. I wondered why Aunt Ruth was coming over on a Sunday morning. She never does.

I was in the bathroom rinsing out my toothbrush when Amy barged in. 'You're supposed to knock,' I told her.

'Karen . . .'

'What?'

'Do you know where Daddy is?'

'You heard Mom,' I said. 'He's busy doing something.'

'I think I know what,' Amy said.

'You do?'

'Yes. I think he's out getting us a puppy and it's supposed to be a big surprise.'

'Where'd you get that idea?'

'In my head.'

'Oh, Amy . . . I don't think that's it at all.' I felt sorry for her then.

Amy sat down on the toilet.

I went into my room and made the bed. When I finished I sat at my desk and opened my Day Book to Sunday, 28 February. I wrote: *Something is going on. I wish I knew what.*

I put the rubber bands back and took out my English homework. I nearly jumped right out of my chair when Aunt Ruth stuck her head in and called, 'Good morning . . .'

She has her own key to our house, so she doesn't have to ring the bell or knock. I never even heard her come in. She can be as sneaky as Mew. She should wear bells around her neck.

'You scared me!' I said.

'I'm sorry,' Aunt Ruth told me. 'Where are Jeff and Amy?'

'Jeff's up in his room and Amy's probably in the den watching TV.' You can't pull Amy away from those dumb Sunday-morning shows. She likes the one where the kids throw pies at each other.

'Where's your mother?' Aunt Ruth asked.

'Getting dressed, I think.'

'Well, suppose you tell Jeff and Amy to get ready and I'll tell your mother I'm here.'

'Get ready for what?'

'Didn't your mother tell you?'

'Tell me what?'

'Uncle Dan and I are taking you out to lunch.'

'But we just had breakfast.'

'We're going for a ride in the country, Karen. By the time we get there it will be lunchtime. So get your coat and tell Jeff and Amy to hurry and get ready.'

'Okay,' I said. We never go out to lunch on Sunday. Sometimes we go out for dinner, but *never* lunch. We don't even eat lunch on Sunday. And Aunt Ruth knows it!

'Aunt Ruth . . .' I called as she was leaving my room.

'Yes.'

'Is Mom coming too?'

'Of course.'

'And Daddy?'

'No. He's not coming.'

'Where is he, anyway?'

'He's got some business to take care of,' Aunt Ruth said.

Business? What kind of business would my father do on a Sunday morning? Unless he's selling the store! I'll bet that's it. Didn't he just tell us that sales are way down? So he's going to sell now and

27

get some other kind of job. Jeff is wrong! Mom was upset because this means we'll be very poor. She might have to hock all her antiques. I'll get a job after school, to help out. Maybe I can deliver newspapers.

I ran downstairs and found Amy in the den. She was wearing her underwear. The rest of her clothes were spread out on the floor. I told her to hurry up and get dressed.

Then I went into the laundry room to check Mew's litter box. It was clean and I was glad. I rinsed her bowl and gave her fresh water. I filled her dish up with dried food. I didn't know how long we'd be gone and I wanted to make sure she wouldn't get hungry. She prefers canned cat food but I'm not allowed to leave that in her dish all day.

When I open a *can* of food for Mew I have to hold my nose. It really stinks. So does her litter box sometimes. But I have discovered that if you love someone the way I love Mew, you learn to overlook the disgusting things. And when I hold her close and she purrs at me it's all worth it.

When we were settled in the car Aunt Ruth drove down to her house to pick up Uncle Dan. Then they switched places so Uncle Dan could drive. We rode all the way to Basking Ridge with Jeff, Amy and me in the back of the car. And when Uncle Dan drives he moves the front seat as far back as it goes because of his long legs. Which means whoever is sitting in the back gets squashed.

Aunt Ruth and Uncle Dan talked the whole time. About the weather and what a nice day it was and how it was just perfect for a drive and how all the snow melted since last week and that there is only one month to go until spring. When Aunt Ruth said that, she put her arm around my mother and added, 'Everything will look brighter in the spring, Ellie.'

Jeff leaned close and whispered, 'You see . . . what did I tell you?'

'It's not what you think,' I whispered back. I couldn't tell him in front of everyone that what Aunt Ruth meant was that then the store will be sold and Daddy will have a new job.

By the time we got to the restaurant Amy was carsick and she threw up in the parking lot. We are used to that. She does it every time we go for a long ride. She is so experienced she never even messes herself up. And she can eat like a tiger afterwards. She never gets sick on the way home – only going. I wonder why?

The restaurant was called the Red Bull Inn and it had bare wooden floors and paper place mats that looked like lace on each table. I studied the menu. Our waitress recommended the curried shrimp. Jeff, Amy and I ordered hamburgers and french fries. My mother said she'd have an omelet and Aunt Ruth and Uncle Dan said they would try the curried shrimp. The waitress seemed really glad to hear that, as if she had been cooking all day and now at last somebody was going to eat her stuff.

When we were almost through, Mom said, 'I have something to tell you.' She wasn't looking at Aunt Ruth or Uncle Dan. She was looking at me and Jeff and Amy. 'I wanted to tell you before, but I just couldn't. It isn't easy for me to say this and it won't be easy for you to understand . . .'

I dropped my fork then. It made a clinking sound when it hit the floor. I bent down to get it.

Uncle Dan said, 'Let it go, Karen. The waitress can bring you another one.'

'Go ahead . . . tell us what you were going to say, Mother,' Jeff said.

Mom took a deep breath and said, 'Daddy and I are separating.'

'I knew it!' Jeff said, looking at me.

I felt tears come to my eyes. I told myself, don't start crying now Karen, you jerk. *Not now.* I sniffled and took a long swallow of Coke. I guess I knew it all the time. I was just fooling myself – playing games like Amy.

'What's separating?' Amy asked.

'It means your father isn't going to live at home any more,' Aunt Ruth explained.

'But he has to!' Amy said. 'He's our father.'

'Shush . . .' Aunt Ruth told her. 'Everyone can hear.'

'I don't care,' Amy shouted, looking around the restaurant. But there were only a few other customers.

Uncle Dan reached for Amy's hand. 'Sometimes, when a mother and father have problems, they live apart for a while to think things over.'

'Is he coming back?' Jeff asked. 'Or are you getting a divorce?'

'We don't know yet,' Mom told him.

'A divorce!' I said, when I hadn't planned to say anything. 'You wouldn't! You wouldn't get a divorce!' Then I started crying for real and I jumped up from the table and ran through the restaurant. I heard Aunt Ruth call, 'Karen . . . Karen . . . come back here.' But I kept going. I didn't want to hear any more. I went out the front door and stood against the sign that said Red Bull Inn, letting the tears roll down my face.

Soon Aunt Ruth came with my coat. 'Karen,' she said, 'put this on. You'll freeze to death.'

'Go away,' I told her.

Aunt Ruth wrapped the coat around my shoulders. 'Karen . . . don't be like that. This is even harder on your mother than it is on you. She's very upset . . . if she sees you like this it's going to make her feel even worse.'

You don't argue with Aunt Ruth. She has a

31

habit of not listening to anything she doesn't want to hear. So I put on my coat and Aunt Ruth said, 'Now, that's better.'

We walked through the parking lot to the car. Aunt Ruth kept her arm around me. 'Nothing is settled yet,' she said. 'Your father is home packing his things now. That's why we all went out to lunch. To give him a chance to move.'

'But doesn't he want to see us? Doesn't he care? How can he move out of his own house?'

'Karen . . . there are some things that are very hard for children to understand.'

That's what people say when they can't explain something to you. I don't believe it. I can understand anything they can understand. I got into the car but I didn't say anything else. I looked out the side window.

'You have to be the one to help your mother,' Aunt Ruth said. 'She needs you . . . more than ever.'

I shook my head and pressed my forehead against the window. Why did Jeff have to be right? Why couldn't it have been something else? If only we could go back a few days and start again maybe things would work out differently.

My mother came out of the restaurant with Amy and Jeff. Mom was carrying an ice cream cone. 'Here, Karen,' she said. 'I know you like dessert best.'

I tried to smile at Mom because I couldn't say thank you. I knew if I said anything I'd start crying. I didn't want the cone, even though it was coffee, my favourite flavour. But I took it from Mom and licked it anyway.

'Dan will be right out,' Mom told Aunt Ruth. 'He's paying the bill.'

'Shove over, Karen,' Jeff said.

'No, I like it here,' I told him. 'Get in on the other side.'

'I said shove over!' Jeff repeated.

When I didn't, he climbed across me and stepped on my foot. I kicked him as hard as I could. He gave me an elbow in the ribs and my ice cream landed in my lap.

Chapter 6

What will happen to me if they get divorced? Who will I live with? Where will I go to school? Will my friends laugh? I want a mother and a father and I want them to live together – right here – in this house! I don't care if they fight. I would rather have them fight than be divorced. I'm scared . . . I'm so scared. I wish somebody would talk to me and tell me it's going to be all right. I miss Daddy already. I hate them both! I wish I was dead.

On Monday morning I didn't get up. My mother came into my room to see what was wrong. 'I'm sick,' I told her. 'I can't go to school.'

Mom sat down on my bed. 'I know how you feel about me and Daddy . . .'

'It's not that,' I said. 'I wasn't even thinking about you. It's my head and my stomach. I might throw up.'

Mom put her hand on my forehead. 'You don't feel warm.'

'A person can be very sick without a fever,' I said.

'You're right,' she told me. 'I better call Dr Winters.'

'Don't bother,' I said. 'I just want to sleep.'

'Well . . . okay. But if you get any worse I'll have to call him.'

'If I can just sleep I'll feel better.'

'All right.'

I heard Jeff and Amy getting ready for school. How can they go? How can they face their friends? I heard my mother calling, 'Amy . . . Amy . . . hurry up or you'll miss the bus.' Some things never change, I thought.

I stayed in bed all day. My mother made me tea and toast but I wouldn't eat it. Later she tried soup but I wouldn't eat that either. She said if I didn't take something she'd have to call the doctor. So I drank some juice.

Debbie stopped by after school, on the way to her piano lesson. She came upstairs and stood in the doorway of my room.

'Hi,' she said. 'What's wrong?'

'Everything,' I told her. She looked pretty. Her cheeks were all pink from the cold. I wanted to tell her about my mother and father. I wanted to tell her so bad it made my head hurt for real. But I couldn't. Saying it would make it come true.

Debbie sat down on my other bed. 'Your mother said it's not catching so it's all right for me to be in your room.'

'My mother told you it's not catching?' I asked.

'Yes.'

'Well, I'd like to know how she can say that.'

'I don't know,' Debbie said, 'but she did. You look like you've been crying.'

'So? Maybe I have been. Don't you ever cry when you're sick?'

'No,' Debbie said.

'Well, this is an unusual sickness. It makes you cry!'

'Why are you mad at me?' Debbie asked.

'I'm not,' I said. 'I just don't feel like talking. Can't you see . . . I'm sick!'

'Want me to make monkey faces for you?'

'No – not today.' Debbie can make very good monkey faces. She can look like a chimpanzee or a gorilla. Usually I crack up when she does them. But I didn't feel like laughing today.

'Will you be back in school tomorrow?' Debbie asked.

'No. I'll be out a long, long time. I may never get better.'

'Oh, come on, Karen! You want me to bring you your books?'

'I've got my English book home.'

'How about maths?'

'No . . . I don't want it.'

'Should I tell Mrs Singer what's wrong with you?'

'No. Don't tell her anything!'

Debbie looked at the floor. I turned away from

her and faced the wall. After a minute she said, 'Is Jeff home yet?'

'How should I know? I'm in bed. Can't you see that?'

'I was just wondering . . . that's all.'

'He doesn't like you anyway, so why don't you just leave him alone.'

'Did he say that?' Debbie asked.

'He doesn't have to. Anyone with eyes can see it. And who did you come here to see anyway . . . me or him?' I was making Debbie feel bad and I was glad. Sometimes I am a mean and rotten person.

Debbie jumped up. 'I came to see *you* and you know it! Whatever's wrong with you I hope it goes away soon because it's making you imposs- ible!' Debbie walked to the door. 'I'm going.'

'So go!' I told her.

'I am.'

Lying to Debbie did not make me feel any better. It made me feel worse.

Later Mom came into my room and told me to put on my bath-robe and come downstairs for dinner.

'I don't want anything to eat,' I said.

'Karen, if you don't get up and come down you can't go to school tomorrow.'

'So?'

'If you don't go to school tomorrow, you won't be able to have dinner with Daddy.'

I sat up. 'He's coming back?'

'No. He's taking you and Jeff and Amy out to eat. He wants to talk to you.'

'Who says I want to talk to him?' I asked.

'Karen . . . don't be like that! Daddy is a wonderful person. He loves you.'

'If he's so wonderful why are you separated?'

'Because we can't get along,' Mom said.

'You could try!' I told her, feeling a lump in my throat.

'We have tried. Now I don't want to talk about it any more.'

I put on my bath-robe and went down for dinner. I wonder if anyone will ever talk about it!

Chapter 7

Debbie was really surprised to see me at the bus stop the next morning. 'I thought you were very sick,' she said.

'I was. But I got better.'

'So fast?' she asked.

'Yes. It was one of those twenty-four-hour bugs.'

'Oh.'

'Hey, look, Debbie . . . I'm really sorry I acted that way yesterday. It was just that my head was killing me and all . . .'

'Forget it,' Debbie said.

'Did I miss much in school?' I asked.

'No. Same old thing. Mrs Singer changed our desks around. I'm next to Gary Owens and Eileen.'

'Where am I?'

'I'm not sure. But I think you're next to the wall on one side.'

'That figures,' I said. 'One more way for Mrs Singer to get me.'

'I really don't think she's out to get you,' Debbie said.

'Ha-ha.'

'I mean it, Karen. You know I can't stand her either, but I don't think she treats you any worse than the rest of us.'

'Well, I do.'

When we got to school I handed Mrs Singer my note from home. It said: *Please excuse Karen's absence on Monday. She wasn't feeling well.*

Mrs Singer said, 'I'm glad you're feeling better, Karen.'

I looked at her. Did she know something? Did my mother call the school and tell them about Daddy moving out? Why else would Mrs Singer act nice all of a sudden? She never says anything when you've been absent. One time Debbie was sick for a couple of weeks and when she came back to school Mrs Singer didn't even smile. So why should she be glad I'm feeling better? If she knows the truth about my parents I will absolutely die.

My father called for us at five that night. He didn't come inside. He just tooted his horn. Amy ran out of the house first. 'Daddy . . . Daddy . . . Daddy . . .' she yelled. Jeff and I followed. We got into the car and said, 'Hi.'

We went to Howard Johnson's on the highway. We sat in a booth in the back room and my father ordered a Martini. You have to sit in that section if you're going to have a drink. It was pretty quiet in the dining room. Maybe because it was so early or maybe because it was Tuesday night. Monday and Wednesday are the Big Fish Fry and Big

Chicken Fry nights, where you can eat all you want for $1.98.

I can't remember ever eating out with just Daddy and not Mom too. I think we all felt funny. I know I did. There I was with my own father and it was like I hadn't seen him for ages instead of just a few days. He looked the same. I didn't expect him not to. But I thought there'd be something different about him now. I don't know what. But something that would let people know he didn't live at home any more.

After we ordered, Daddy said, 'I miss you all very much.'

Me and Jeff mumbled that we missed him too.

Then Amy asked, 'Do you miss Mommy?'

My father looked sad and said, 'No, I don't.'

'Are you getting a divorce?' Jeff asked.

'Yes,' my father answered.

'I thought you were just thinking about it,' I said. 'I thought it wasn't definite yet.'

'We're definitely getting a divorce,' he said. 'It's the only way.'

'Do you love somebody else?' Jeff asked. 'Or does Mom?'

I never even thought about that! I couldn't picture my father with another woman or my mother with another man. That was disgusting! How could Jeff even think of such a thing? I took a sip of water and waited for my father to answer.

41

'No . . . no . . .' he said. 'It's nothing like that. There's nobody else involved. Your mother and I just don't get along. We can't go on living together. It's making a mess of our lives.'

'Suppose we don't want you to get a divorce?' I said.

'I'm sorry, Karen, but this is between your mother and me.'

'I want to live with you, Daddy!' Amy said.

'Don't be a jerk,' Jeff told Amy. 'The kids always live with the mother.'

'Is that true?' I asked.

'Yes, usually,' Daddy said. 'Unless there's some reason why the mother shouldn't have the children.'

'What about us?' I asked. 'Where will we live?'

'With your mother.'

'But where?'

'Right now you'll stay in the house.'

'But for how long?' I asked.

'Karen . . . you're asking me questions I can't answer,' Daddy said. 'We haven't worked out any of the details yet. I'm seeing my lawyer tomorrow. You don't get divorced overnight.'

'How long does it take?' Jeff asked.

'That depends. I guess about six months. Maybe more.'

'Daddy . . .' Amy said, 'please come home.'

My father held Amy to him. Then he took off

his glasses and started to clean them with his napkin. I think he had tears in his eyes. I didn't feel like eating anything.

After dinner Daddy took us into the motel to see his room. It has two beds and a TV. The bathroom is very small. 'Are you going to live here forever?' I asked.

'No. Just until I find an apartment.'

'Will we still see you?' I said.

'Of course you will. I'm your father and I'll always love you. Divorce has nothing to do with that.'

After a few minutes Jeff said, 'Well . . . I've got to get home. I have lots of homework to do.' His voice broke on every word.

Nobody said much on the drive back to our house. When we got there Amy asked Daddy to come in and carry her up to bed like he always does. But Daddy said, 'No, I'm not coming in.'

Tuesday, 2 March
Divorce . . . it's the end of the world.

Chapter 8

In the middle of the night Amy shook me. I sat straight up in bed. 'What's the matter?' I asked.

'I'm afraid to go to sleep,' she said.

'Why?'

'I'm afraid if I do you'll all be gone in the morning, just like Daddy.'

'That's silly,' I told her.

She threw her arms around me. She was shaking. I held her tight. 'Can I sleep in here with you?' she asked.

'I guess so,' I said. But I really didn't want her to. I wanted to be alone. How could I cry with Amy in my other bed?

As soon as I tucked her in she fell asleep. But I tossed and turned for a long time. I wish I could talk to somebody about my parents. If only Debbie knew – I think I would feel better. I've got to figure out a way to tell her what's happening. She'll be able to cheer me up. Besides making monkey faces, Debbie has a very good sense of humour. I guess that's why everybody likes her. She doesn't even mind laughing at herself. I'm really lucky to have her for a best friend, even though I don't always show it. I am sure just having her know the truth will help.

On Wednesday afternoons Debbie and I walk to Girl Scouts together. Our troop meets at Willow Grove Church. That's just a few blocks from school. Then either Debbie's mother or mine picks us up. I used to love my Girl Scout uniform. But I am thinking of quitting after this year. So is Debbie. We are both sick of selling cookies and calendars to the same people year after year. If we had a good leader it would be different. But ours is a bore. If I was ever going to be a Girl Scout leader I would think up interesting activities for my group to do. And if they made a lot of noise I wouldn't yell that they give me a headache.

I planned to tell Debbie about my parents while we were walking to our meeting. But by three o'clock I was so mad at Mrs Singer I couldn't think of anything else! Because this afternoon she called me up to her desk to discuss this month's book report. It was due last Monday. I scribbled mine out Sunday night before I went to sleep. I never even read the book. I just copied some stuff off the inside flap of the jacket. I've never done that before, but some kids in my class do it all the time.

Mrs Singer said, 'Did you enjoy the book you read this month, Karen?'

I said, 'It was all right.'

'Your book report wasn't nearly as good as usual.'

45

'I was very busy,' I told her. 'I had to do it in a hurry.'

'What did you think about the ending?'

'It was all right.'

'Were you surprised by it?'

'A little,' I said. I could tell that Mrs Singer knew I hadn't read the book. Just as the bell rang she handed me my book report. I got a D – my first bad mark in school.

I could feel my face turn red as I walked to the back of the room to get my coat. Debbie waited for me at her desk. I picked up my books and marched out into the hall. Debbie called, 'Goodbye, Mrs Singer,' as she followed me.

Mrs Singer called back, 'Goodbye, girls.'

I didn't answer her.

When we were out of the building Debbie asked, 'What's wrong?'

'Nothing!'

'What'd Mrs Singer want to see you for?'

'Don't mention that witch's name! I hate her!'

'What'd she do?'

'Gave me a D on my book report!'

'She did?'

'Yes. There's something about me that Mrs Singer can't stand. This proves it!'

'She hardly ever gives out Ds for book reports,' Debbie said, 'unless she thinks you didn't read the book.'

I glared at Debbie, then I pulled my scarf up around my face. The wind was howling and it was really cold. We hurried along not saying anything for a while.

We only had one more block to go when Debbie said, 'I heard about your parents . . . and I'm sorry.'

'Heard what?' I asked, biting my lip.

'You know.'

'Know what?'

'Oh, come on, Karen. That your parents are getting a divorce.'

Well, there it was. Out in the open. But not the way I'd planned it. *I* was the one who was going to tell Debbie. And *she* was the one who was going to make me feel better. 'Who told you?' I asked.

'Your aunt met my mother in Food Town and she told her.'

'Oh,' I said. I always knew Aunt Ruth had a big mouth. It must have to do with her rabbit teeth. She's just like Amy.

'How come you didn't tell me?' Debbie asked when we got to the church.

'It wasn't definite.' We went inside and jumped around a little to get warm. Then we hung up our coats. 'What's it like?' Debbie asked.

'What do you mean?'

'What's it feel like?'

How could she ask such a dumb question! 'How do you think it feels?' I said, running for the bathroom.

'Hey, Karen . . . wait up!' Debbie caught me before I got inside. 'I'm sorry. I didn't know it would be so bad.'

'Well, it is.'

'Are they going to have a fight over you and Jeff and Amy?'

'What kind of fight?'

'You know . . . about who gets the kids.'

'No. We stay with our mother.'

'Doesn't your father want you?'

'I don't know. He said we'll live with our mother.' Now I was getting all mixed up. Why did she ask if Daddy wanted us? Did Aunt Ruth know something else? Did she tell Mrs Bartell something that Debbie knows? Oh . . . I hate everybody! I must have been crazy to think Debbie could cheer me up.

Chapter 9

I have only one grandparent and that's Daddy's father. We call him Garfa because Jeff couldn't say 'Grandpa' when he was a baby. When you are twelve you feel pretty stupid calling somebody Garfa, especially in public. So whenever I talk about him in school or to my friends I say 'my grandfather'. Only Debbie knows he is Garfa.

Garfa started Newman's furniture store when he was young, in the olden days. Daddy took it over thirteen years ago when Grandma died and Garfa retired. I never knew my grandmother but everybody says I look like her. I've seen some pictures though and I don't think there is any resemblance between us at all. But you can't argue about something like that with your family. Once they make up their minds that you look like somebody special, that's it.

Garfa lives in Las Vegas. The dry climate is supposed to be good for his health. But I have heard that he likes gambling. This is not something that the family talks about much. Last year Garfa got married again. His new wife's name is Mattie and she is sixty-five years old. Imagine getting married when you are sixty-five!

Garfa and Mattie visited us over the summer.

The only thing wrong with Mattie is she doesn't like cats. She more than doesn't like them – she is terrified of them. So Debbie kept Mew at her house for two whole weeks.

I just found out that Garfa is going to pay us a visit this weekend, but Mattie is staying home in Las Vegas. Daddy called to tell him about the divorce, which is why he is coming.

On Saturday, Garfa came into our house alone. Daddy just dropped him off. The first thing Garfa said after he kissed us and gave us the once-over was, 'Well, Ellie, there hasn't ever been a divorce in our family. Not even way back. When the Newmans get married they get married for keeps. Or until one of them dies.'

My mother didn't say anything. She just shook her head. I didn't think Garfa should discuss the divorce in front of Amy. But of course he didn't know she was so afraid at night.

'Listen, Ellie . . . everybody has problems,' Garfa said. 'Even me and Mattie have problems. But we're willing to work them out. That's what you have to do. Work out your problems with Bill.'

'We can't,' my mother said.

'Dammit, Ellie! Don't give me that! Of course you can. That's why I came. I want you and Bill to get away for a little while. All you need is a vacation. And it's on me.'

'Oh, Garfa . . .' Mom said. 'Thank you for trying but it's just no use. A vacation isn't going to solve anything. Don't you see . . .' Mom ran upstairs.

Later, after Daddy picked up Garfa, my mother drove downtown to get a box of Kentucky Fried Chicken for supper. Daddy can't stand that stuff. Well, now he'll never have to eat it.

I set the table while Mom cut up the salad. I didn't put out our regular paper napkins. I went into the den and came back with some of the cocktail napkins that say *Ellie and Bill*. I folded them up and put one at each place.

My mother called Jeff and Amy for supper. She didn't see the napkins until we were all seated. Then she looked at me and said, 'I don't think this is very funny, Karen.'

'I wasn't trying to be funny,' I said.

'Then why did you use these?'

'Because there isn't going to be any more Ellie and Bill and I thought we might as well use them up now.'

Mom collected the napkins and mashed them into a ball. She got up from the table and threw them away. 'Where's the rest of the box?' she asked me.

'In the den, by the bar.'

'Okay . . . after dinner get it and put it in the garbage.'

'Boy, are you stupid!' Jeff whispered to me.

My mother didn't eat any chicken. I don't think she's been eating anything lately. She is getting very skinny. If she is so miserable without Daddy and he is so miserable away from us then why are they getting divorced? I don't understand.

On Sunday night Daddy took us out to dinner. We went to The Towers Steak House, which is my all-time favourite restaurant. I have never eaten out as much as in the week my parents have been separated.

During dinner Garfa tried to persuade Daddy to take a vacation with Mom. But it didn't work. Daddy said that was out of the question.

I could see how disappointed Garfa was at not being able to get my parents back together, so when we were alone for a minute I said, 'Don't worry, Garfa.' I thought of telling him about that TV show where the little boy got kidnapped. But I didn't. Because those things never happen in real life, do they?

'I can't help it, Karen,' Garfa said. 'I was so sure I'd be able to straighten everything out.'

'Do you think I should try too?' I asked.

Garfa smiled at me. 'It can't hurt.'

Before he flew home to Las Vegas, Garfa told me to keep him posted on whatever was going on. 'You're the most dependable person in this family,

Karen. You're just like your Grandmother Newman. And you know something? You look more
like her every time I see you.'

'Oh, Garfa!' was all I could think to say.

Chapter 10

Petey Mansfield seems to have moved into our house. He is Jeff's new best friend. They're always locked up inside Jeff's hideaway.

I don't know if Petey Mansfield is normal or not. He doesn't talk at all. Sometimes if you ask him a question he'll grunt at you, but otherwise, forget it. How does he manage in school? I wonder. His brother Brian is in my class. He never shuts up. Mrs Singer is always yelling at him. Maybe that's why Petey doesn't talk. Maybe he doesn't ever get a chance.

Eileen Fenster, who is a girl in my class, says Brian Mansfield likes me. She knows because she spends every afternoon calling up boys. She asks them questions such as 'Who do you like in our class?' or 'What do you think of Debbie?' or something like that.

Debbie and I went over to Eileen's a few times. She knows all the boys' phone numbers by heart. The last time I was there she called up Gary Owens and I listened on the upstairs phone. She said, 'Hi Gary. This is Eileen. Listen, Gary . . . what do you think of Karen?'

And Gary said, 'Karen who?'

Imagine him saying that! How many Karens does he know anyway?

So Eileen said, 'Karen Newman.'

And Gary said, 'Oh, her.'

'Well?' Eileen said.

And then Gary hung up! Why did he go and do that? I'm never going to Eileen's house again.

Aunt Ruth came over tonight. She was full of advice for my mother because tomorrow is Mom's first meeting with Mr Hague, her lawyer.

We were sitting around the kitchen table. Aunt Ruth and Mom were drinking coffee and I was eating a banana. I only like bananas when they are pure yellow, without a spot of brown. That's why I hardly ever eat them.

Aunt Ruth said, 'What are you going to wear tomorrow?'

And Mom said, 'I don't know. What difference does it make?'

Aunt Ruth said, 'You want to make a good impression, don't you? And remember, Ellie, you've got to tell him everything, no matter how hard it is for you.'

'I know,' my mother said. 'Dan told me the same thing.'

'I wish you'd try to eat a little more, Ellie. You don't look well.'

'Oh, Ruth . . .' Mom said.

'I don't want to interfere, Ellie . . . I just wish you'd take better care of yourself.'

Aunt Ruth is right. Suppose my mother gets sick? Then who'll take care of us?

Nobody said anything for a minute. Then Aunt Ruth asked Mom, 'Do you remember Henry Farnum?'

'I think so,' Mom said. 'Is he the accountant?'

'That's the one,' Aunt Ruth said. 'From West Orange. Dan and I ran into him the other day. You know his wife died last year . . .'

'No, I didn't know that,' Mom said.

'Yes . . . he's been very lonely. He's got a beautiful house and nobody in it. His children are both away at college.'

'He ought to move to an apartment,' Mom said.

I got up and threw my banana skin away.

'I'd like you to meet him, Ellie.'

'Oh, please, Ruth . . . don't start in on that.'

I sat back down at the table. Start in on what?

'Look, Ellie . . . that's the wrong attitude to take. Here I know a really nice man. He's lonely. So what's wrong with going out to dinner with him? I'm not saying you've got to marry him.'

'Ruth, please! I'm not even divorced yet. I don't want to think about getting married again.'

'Okay. Fine. But a year from now when Henry Farnum is married to somebody else, don't come crying to me. And don't tell me you think Bill is sitting home alone every night!'

'Ruth . . . not in front of Karen . . . please.'

Aunt Ruth looked at me. Does she know something? Why doesn't she just stay home and mind her own business! I hope my mother never goes out with Mr Henry Farnum or any other man!

On Friday there was no school because of some special teachers' meeting. Debbie and I decided to go ice-skating. There is a pond in the middle of town, next to the library. When the blue circle is up it means the pond is frozen and safe to skate on.

Debbie's mother called for me and drove us downtown. I felt funny because Mrs Bartell knows about my parents. I was scared that she would ask me something and I wouldn't know what to tell her. But she didn't mention one word about the divorce. She talked about keeping warm instead. And how she wanted Debbie to wear a few pairs of underpants instead of just one. 'That's the best way to get a kidney infection,' Mrs Bartell said, 'sitting on that cold ice and getting a chill.'

'I promise I won't sit on the ice,' Debbie said.

I think Mrs Bartell spends a lot of time worrying about diseases. She dropped us off right in front of the library and we walked down the path to the pond. There was already a bunch of kids there. I saw Eileen Fenster right away. She waved.

I love to ice-skate. I learned by myself when I was nine. That year I got my first shoe skates for Christmas. Debbie is always joking about her ice-skating lessons. She says it took her one whole year just to learn to stand up on the ice.

We were already wearing our skates, so all we had to do was to take the covers off the blades and skate away. I don't think Debbie was on the pond for two minutes before she fell down. I pulled her up. She started to laugh. 'Three years of lessons and I still stink!' she said. Then I started to laugh too. Eileen Fenster skated over to see what was so funny and pretty soon we were all standing there laughing. I had forgotten how good it feels to laugh. From now on I am going to concentrate on laughing at least once a day – even more if I can arrange it.

After an hour I could see why Mrs Bartell wanted Debbie to wear lots of underpants. She wound up sitting on the ice more than she was standing on it! I skated out to the middle of the pond to practise my figure eights. When I turned around to look for Debbie I saw her standing on the grass talking to Eileen. I waved and called, 'Hey, Debbie . . .' but she didn't notice. What were they talking about that was so important? Were they telling secrets? Was Eileen saying something bad about me? I skated across to them and said, 'What's up?'

As soon as they saw me they stopped talking. Eileen said, 'Oh, nothing. Me and Debbie were just saying it's fun to have a day off from school.'

I knew that wasn't the truth. I could tell from their faces.

After Eileen went home I asked Debbie, 'What were you talking about before?'

'Nothing,' Debbie said. 'Just forget it.'

'I'll bet it was about me.'

'Okay . . . so it was.'

'About me and Gary Owens . . . right?'

'No. About your parents, if you want to hear the truth.'

'My parents?'

'Yes. Eileen just found out they're getting divorced.'

'Oh.' I took my chapstick out of my pocket and rubbed some along my bottom lip.

'You can't keep it a secret,' Debbie said. 'Sooner or later everyone is going to know.'

'I never said it was a secret.'

'Well, anyway . . . that's what we were talking about.'

'What did Eileen say?'

'Oh, she was just asking me if your mother has a lot of money, that's all.'

'Money? What's money got to do with it?'

59

'I don't know exactly. But Eileen heard her mother say that she hopes your mother has a good lawyer and plenty of money.'

'I think Mrs Fenster should mind her own business,' I said.

'Well, so do I! Come on, now . . . just forget about it.' Debbie made her chimpanzee face. I tried to laugh.

But I spent the rest of the day thinking about what Eileen had said. My mother has no money that I know of, unless Aunt Ruth and Uncle Dan are going to give her some. It's scary to think about my mother with no money to feed us or buy our clothes or anything. Maybe we will eat at Aunt Ruth's every night. And instead of giving all our outgrown clothes to some poor family someone will give their old clothes to us. I've got to talk to somebody about this. Maybe Jeff can explain things to me.

Chapter 11

Trying to get to talk to Jeff is like banging your head against the wall. You just don't get anywhere. I've been tagging along after him for three days now but he says he's very busy and I should get lost. I think Petey Mansfield is a bad influence on him. I would tell that to my mother but suppose she says, 'Why are you so anxious to have a private talk with Jeff?' What can I possibly answer without giving everything away?

I have come up with some information, though. From now on my father will be taking us out to dinner every Wednesday night and we will spend Sunday afternoons with him. This is part of something called a separation agreement. Daddy's lawyer's name is Mr Levinson and he specializes in divorces just like Mr Hague. Their offices are even in the same building in Newark. I wonder if maybe my mother and father will run into each other there.

Divorce is a very complicated thing. I always thought if you wanted one you just got it. But now I know that sometimes you need special reasons and each state has different rules. Uncle Dan explained this to me the other night. When I got into bed I thought of a million questions I should have asked him, like suppose I am sick on a Wednesday and can't go out to eat. Does that mean I don't get to see Daddy at all? I have *got* to talk to Jeff. If it takes me a week I am going to corner him. I will station myself outside the bathroom door when he is inside and I will not move until he comes out. There will be no way he can ignore me.

It didn't take me a week. On the second night, I sat down cross-legged right in front of the locked bathroom door. I listened as Jeff brushed his teeth and took a shower. When he opened the door he was really surprised to find me there waiting. He had a towel wrapped around himself and his hair was all wet.

'What are you doing?' he asked me.

'Waiting to talk to you.'

'I'm busy,' he said.

'I can wait.' I wanted to say, 'Please talk to me – I need somebody so bad.' I felt tears come to my eyes. I think Jeff noticed.

He said, 'Okay . . . go up and wait for me in the hideaway. I'll be right there. And here' – he handed me a tissue – 'blow your nose.'

I took it and ran up the stairs. I opened the door to his hideaway and sat down on his bed to wait. There was a picture of Mary Louise Rumberger tacked up on his bulletin board. She was wearing a bathing suit. She's pretty hefty.

When Jeff came up he was wearing a bath-robe and his hair was still wet but he had combed it. 'What's wrong?' he asked.

'Does Mom have any money?' I said.

'What do you mean?'

'I mean does she have any money of her own . . . that's not Daddy's.'

'I don't know,' Jeff said. 'I never thought about it. Why?'

'Because if she doesn't, what do you think is going to happen to us?'

'I think they make some kind of deal when they get divorced. Dad pays a certain amount of money to Mom every month. Something like that.'

'Are you sure?' I asked.

'He's not going to let us starve, if that's what you're worried about.'

'You're sure about that?'

'Yes, I'm sure. But if you don't believe me why don't you ask him yourself?'

'That's a very good idea. I think I'll do that. And another thing,' I said.

'Go on . . .'

'Well, suppose I get sick and can't go to see him at all?'

'How am I supposed to know about that? You're thinking too much about the divorce.'

'Do you mean you never think about it?'

'Well, sure I do. But we'll probably see more of Dad now than we did before.'

'I don't care,' I said. 'It's not the same as having a father living at home where he belongs!' I started to cry again.

'You just better get used to it Karen,' Jeff said in a funny voice. 'Because there's nothing you can do about it!'

That's what he thinks! I'm going to get them back together. I told Garfa I'd try, didn't I?

Chapter 12

Friday, 26 March
My life is going from bad to worse!

I found out today that Gary Owens is moving to Houston. His father has been transferred there. I wonder if he will start to like me before he moves? Probably not.

I forgot my milk money again. Mrs Singer wants to know what's wrong with me. I told her nothing. Debbie said her parents bumped into my father at the Chinese restaurant. He was all alone, so the Bartells invited him to join them. Debbie said her mother told her not to tell me this – but my father is very lonely and unhappy. Why did she have to go and tell me?

If one more bad thing happens I just don't know what I am going to do!

My mother went to see Mr Hague today for the second time. And when she came home she had a new haircut, a new dress and a smile on her face. So right away I thought, she's in love. Because I've been thinking a lot about that lately. Jeff says he is positive that Daddy and Mom are not too old for that stuff. I wonder!

Mom was in her room changing into a sweater

and a pair of pants. I sat on her bed. 'What's Mr Hague like?'

'Who?' she asked from inside her sweater.

This time I waited until her head was all the way through. 'Mr Hague,' I said. 'What's he like?'

'Oh . . . he's very nice. He's going to take care of everything.' She fluffed out her hair.

'Do you want to marry him?'

'Marry who?'

'Mr Hague.'

'For heaven's sake, Karen! I've only seen him twice. And he's already married, with five kids.'

'How do you know that?'

'I saw a picture of his family on his desk.'

'Oh. Then you're not in love?'

'No, I'm not. And what's all this *love* business anyway?'

'I don't know,' I said. 'You seem so happy today.'

'Well, I am. It's a relief to know that soon everything will be settled.'

'Mom . . .'

'Yes?'

'Will you tell me *exactly* why you're getting divorced?'

'Oh, Karen! We've been through this before.'

'But there has to be a reason.'

'There isn't any reason.'

'How can there not be a reason? Is it a secret? Is that it? Something I shouldn't know about?'

'No . . . no . . .'

'Well then . . . what?'

'I mean there isn't just one reason. It's not that simple. There are so many reasons. It's just better this way that's all.'

'Does it have anything to do with your antiques?'

'Of course not. Whatever gave you that idea?'

'Oh, I don't know. Because the store sells modern furniture and you like old things.'

Mom laughed a little. 'Daddy likes antiques too. It just happens that his business is selling modern furniture.'

'Well . . . does it have to do with the way you cook, then?'

'Oh, Karen!'

'Daddy's always saying you should try more recipes.'

'But people don't get divorced over those things. You're all mixed up, aren't you?'

'I don't know,' I said. 'I guess I am.'

Mom sat down next to me and took my hand. 'I wish it was easier for you to understand. Daddy and I just don't enjoy being together. We don't love each other any more. We love you and Amy and Jeff just the same, but not each other.'

I took my hand away and fiddled with my chain belt.

'You're going to be a lot happier living in a house without constant fighting,' Mom said.

I didn't say anything.

'You are, Karen. You'll see.'

I nodded. If she was so sure, how come I didn't know it?

'Now let's go down to the kitchen and get dinner ready,' Mom said.

We went downstairs together. Mew was on her favourite chair, bathing. She spends more time licking herself clean every day than I spend in the bath tub in a week.

Chapter 13

On Sunday my father called for us at noon. Mom never comes to the door when she knows Daddy is outside. I don't know how I am going to get them back together when they never even see each other.

We went to visit Daddy's new apartment. He moved this week. The place is called Country Village and it has the kind of streets running through it where you can get lost pretty easy because everything looks the same. There are two swimming pools. One for Country Village East and one for Country Village West. My father's apartment is in West. Each section has four apartments. Daddy's is in building 12, upstairs on the right. It's all fixed up like a magazine picture. Everything is brown-and-white and very modern. The kind of stuff that Newman's Furniture Store sells.

'Well . . . what do you think?' Daddy asked.

'It's terrific!' Jeff said. 'It's a real man's pad. I'd like to live here myself.'

That reminded me of what Debbie said. That Jeff might not want to be the only male in our house.

'Well, son,' Daddy said, 'you can stay here any

time you want. That sofa opens up and I've got two rollaway beds in the storage room.' He looked at me and Amy.

'I'll bet you're glad you're in the furniture business, right Daddy?' I asked. 'I mean, suppose you had to go out and *buy* all this stuff!'

'I don't exactly get it free, Karen . . . but I do save a lot,' Daddy said.

'Well, that's good,' I told him.

After we saw the apartment there wasn't much to do. Amy sat down on the floor in front of the TV and Jeff looked through my father's magazines. I went in the kitchen for something to drink. Daddy followed me.

'How's your mother?' he asked.

'She's fine and you should see her, Daddy . . . she looks great. She got a new haircut and—'

Daddy didn't let me finish. He said, 'What kind of soda do you want?'

'I don't care,' I said. He opened a Coke.

'Daddy, are you still going to pay for us?' I asked.

'Pay for what?'

'Oh, you know . . . our clothes and food and stuff like that.'

'Of course I am, Karen. The lawyers will arrange for your support, and alimony for your mother.'

'What's alimony?'

'An amount of money I'll be paying your mother every month.'

So Jeff really knew what he was talking about.

'Anyway,' Daddy said, 'who's been putting all these ideas about money into your head?'

'Nobody,' I said. 'I was just wondering.'

'You're sure no one told you to ask me?'

'Of course I'm sure.' Who did Daddy think would tell me that?

'Because there isn't anything for you to worry about. I want to make sure you understand that.'

'Suppose I get sick on a Wednesday or a Sunday and I can't come out with you. Does that mean I won't see you that day?'

'If you're sick I'll come to see you.'

'You'll come up to my room?'

'Of course.'

'But what if Mom is home.'

'Listen, Karen . . . your mother and I aren't going to go out of our way to see each other. But if there's an emergency we won't let our personal feelings interfere. Now promise me you aren't going to worry about anything.'

'I'll try not to,' I said. But I was already thinking about getting sick next Wednesday so Daddy will have to come home. And once he's there he'll stay for dinner. Especially if I have a fever. How can I get myself a good fever? I wonder.

'There's a girl about your age in the apartment

downstairs,' Daddy told me. 'I thought you might like to meet her.'

'Oh . . . I don't know,' I said.

'Her parents are divorced and she lives with her mother. They've been very nice to me since I moved in. I told her you'd be visiting today and she said you should come down. Her name is Val Lewis.'

'Well . . .' I said.

'It might be nice for you to have a friend here.'

'Okay . . . I guess . . . if you think I should . . .'

'It's apartment 12-B, on the left. Do you want me to come with you?'

'No. Did you say her name is Val?'

'Yes. Val Lewis.'

'What's she like?'

'Oh . . . a little taller than you maybe and . . .'

'Not Val,' I said. 'Her mother!'

'Oh. She's a very attractive woman.'

'Better-looking than Mom?' I asked.

'In a different way. Why?' Daddy said.

'Just wondering,' I told him.

I went downstairs and stood outside apartment 12-B. I wasn't sure if I wanted to meet this girl or not. Finally I rang the bell.

Val answered. 'Oh, hi,' she said. 'I'll bet you're Karen.'

'Yes . . . my father told me to come down.'

'Come on in,' Val said.

Daddy was right. She is taller than me. But not much. She has very long black hair and bangs that cover her eyebrows. Her eyes remind me of Mew's. They are the same colour green.

'Excuse the mess,' Val said when I walked into the living room. 'I read the whole *New York Times* every Sunday. From cover to cover. I don't skip an inch!'

'That must take all day,' I said.

'It does. And part of the night too. Let's go into my room.'

I followed Val down the hall. 'My father's only got one bedroom,' I said.

'I know,' Val told me. 'All the apartments on the right have one bedroom and the ones on the left have two.' When we got to Val's room she spread her arms. 'It's small, but it's all mine,' she said, pulling up her bedspread. 'I never make the bed on Sunday,' she explained.

'That's okay,' I said. The bed was up against the wall. There was a pink bulletin board that said *Valerie* on it hanging over the bed. She had a big desk with lots of drawers, plus a rug on the floor shaped like a foot, with toes and everything.

Val pulled her desk chair next to the bed and told me to sit down. 'My mother's asleep,' she said. 'I know she'd like to meet you but she was out very late last night.'

'With my father?' I asked.

'Your father?' Val laughed. 'What gave you that idea?'

'I don't know. I just thought that's what you meant.'

'My mother only goes out with one man. Seymour Chandler. Do you know him?'

'No.'

'He's very rich. My mother wants to marry him. Actually, my mother wants to marry anybody who's very rich.'

'Oh,' I said. I hope my mother won't be like that.

'She and my father have been divorced almost three years. My father lives in San Francisco.'

'Have you been there to visit him?' I asked.

'No . . . I haven't seen him since the divorce. He's a runaround and he drinks too much and his cheques are late every month. Once my mother's lawyer had him picked up for nonsupport.'

'My father isn't anything like that,' I said.

'Sometimes the children are the last to know,' Val told me.

'How did you find out about yours?' I asked.

'Oh . . . my mother spent the whole first year after the divorce telling me what a bum my father is.'

'My mother keeps saying my father is a great person,' I said.

Val laughed and said, 'Uh-oh! Watch out for that.'

'Why? What do you mean?'

'Because she's not being honest with you, that's what.'

'How do you know?' I asked.

'It says so – right here.' Val reached under her bed and came up with a book. She opened it and read, ' "If your mother never says bad things about your father it's because she thinks that it's better for you not to know about your father's faults. She may think that you can only love a person who is perfect." ' Val closed the book. 'You see?' she said.

'What kind of book is that?' I asked.

'It's called *The Boys and Girls Book About Divorce* and it's just for kids like us. A doctor wrote it. I'm his greatest fan. I used to write to him once a week when I first got his book. He even answered me.'

'Did your mother buy it for you?' I asked.

'No. I read about it in *The New York Times* and saved my allowance until I had enough. It's very expensive. It costs $7.95.'

'For just one book?'

'Yes, but it's worth it. You ought to ask your father to get it for you. Wait a minute and I'll write down all the information.' Val got up and went to her desk. She wrote on a piece of notebook paper, then folded it and gave it to me. I put it in my pocket.

Val put the divorce book back under her bed and came up with another. 'Do you know the facts of life?' she asked.

'Yes,' I said.

'Oh. If you didn't I was going to say I'd be glad to tell you. I have a book about that too. See . . .' She showed me the book. It was a lot like the one I read at Debbie's.

'What grade are you in?' Val asked.

'Sixth,' I said.

'I'm in seventh. I was twelve in September.'

'I'm twelve too,' I said. 'We're just a few months apart.'

'In age maybe,' Val said. 'But being in seventh grade makes a big difference. For instance, I wouldn't dream of liking a boy in my class.'

'How come?' I asked, thinking about Gary Owens.

'Seventh grade boys are babies. I like eighth or ninth grade boys.'

'My brother's in ninth grade,' I told her.

'Oh . . . I didn't know you have a brother.'

'Yes, and a little sister too.'

'Then you're the middle child?'

'Yes.'

'Uh-oh! That's bad,' Val said. 'Middle children have all kinds of problems.'

'Says who?' I asked.

'Everybody knows that. You're not the oldest and you're not the youngest. So you wind up with problems. The divorce will be harder on you than on them. But cheer up! I'm an *only* child. I have lots of problems too.'

'Val . . . how do you know so much?' I asked.

'I told you,' she said, 'I read the entire *New York Times* every Sunday!'

Chapter 14

Compared to Val, Debbie doesn't know anything. I don't think she's ever read *The New York Times*. And what does she know about divorce or alimony or support? Not much, that's for sure. It's funny how things can change all of a sudden. Now I have more in common with Val than with Debbie. Oh, we're still best friends but we don't see that much of each other outside school. Especially since Mrs Bartell has decided Debbie needs dramatic lessons. She's going to get them every Saturday afternoon.

Now that Gary Owens has moved to Houston, Mrs Singer's let me move my desk away from the wall and next to Debbie's. She said if there is any talking or giggling between us she will separate us again. It's too bad that Gary moved away without ever knowing that I've spent four whole months thinking about him. If I ever feel that way about a boy again I won't waste time. I'll let him know right off. At least I think I will.

We are studying about the Vikings this month. They were pretty interesting guys, but very mean. When they went into battle they acted absolutely crazy. They killed everybody, including the women and children. But they were smart too. For instance, they built great ships. We are going to make Viking dioramas. That sounds like fun, for a change.

This afternoon I tried to find out if Petey Mansfield talks. I waited until he and Jeff locked themselves up inside the hideaway. Then I crept up the stairs very quietly and stood outside Jeff's room, holding a glass to the wall. I pressed my ear against the bottom of the glass. Eileen told me this is the best way to try to hear something you're not supposed to.

It works too! First I heard them laughing. But then they switched on the record player and that was the end of it. All I got was an earful of music. If you ask me, Petey Mansfield can talk when he feels like it.

Debbie says if only I like Petey we could have a double wedding. Meaning her and Jeff and me and Petey. I told her, 'Ha-ha! I wouldn't marry Petey Mansfield if he was the last boy on earth.' And anyway, I'm not getting married.

My mother is eating again. She goes around the house singing now. I still wonder if she's in love. I would like to get a look at this Mr Hague because my mother has gone to his office a few more times, and once when I answered the phone it was *him*. Last week Val told me that women getting divorces always fall for their lawyers.

Tonight at dinner Mom gave us some big news. 'I'm going back to college,' she said.

Amy practically spit out her lima beans. 'To college?'

'Yes,' Mom said. 'That way I'll be able to get a better job.'

'A job?' Jeff and I said together.

'Yes.'

'You're really getting a job?' Jeff asked.

'I hope so,' Mom told him.

'Doing what?' I asked. 'Refinishing furniture?'

'No,' Mom said. 'That's what I'd like to do but I have to be more practical right now.'

What kind of job will she get? What can she do? Maybe she'll be a cashier in the supermarket. Or maybe she'll be a cocktail waitress. That's what divorced women on TV always turn out to be – cocktail waitresses. Imagine my mother dressed in a skimpy costume! Suppose Debbie comes over while she's getting into her waitress clothes. Debbie will say, 'Why is your mother dressed up like a Bunny?' And I won't tell her the truth. I'll say, 'She's going to a costume party.' Then Debbie will say, 'Oh. She looks cute.' But I'll know that she looks terrible.

'I don't know what kind of job I'm going to get,' Mom said. 'That's why I'm going back to college. To take a course in typing and shorthand. I've signed up for an evening class at Seton Hall too.

In English literature. The term's half over, but I can still learn a lot.'

'English literature!' Jeff said. 'Why?'

'Because I only had one year of college before I got married. I had you when I was just twenty,' she told Jeff. She finished eating her salad. Then she said, 'I think I might like to get my degree. I never really had a chance to find out what I might be able to do.'

'Well, don't let me stop you!' Jeff said. 'I can always go and live with Dad.'

My mother's face turned very red. 'Did he tell you that?'

'He said any time I want to I can stay there.' Jeff stood up. 'At least he's not sorry he had us!' He clomped out of the kitchen and slammed the front door.

Mom pushed her chair away from the table. 'Jeff is wrong,' she told me and Amy. 'You know I'm glad to have you.'

Maybe you are and maybe you're not. Who can tell any more?

Tuesday, 6 April
Can Jeff really move out of our house? That would be awful! Even though I can't stand him sometimes, I would still miss him a lot. I like just knowing he's around.

But the next morning Jeff was back and Mom was furious. She threw our breakfast at us. 'Where were you last night?' she asked him.

'That's my business,' Jeff said.

'Just who do you think you're talking to?' Mom asked. 'From now on you're not to run out at night without telling me first. And I want you home by nine thirty during the week.'

'Says who?' Jeff asked.

'Me!' Mom hollered.

'Since when are you the boss?'

'Jeff . . . stop it!' Mom said. 'What's got into you?'

By the time Jeff left for school my mother was on the verge of tears. But when she saw that he had forgotten his lunch she ran after him calling, 'Jeff . . . Jeff . . . you forgot your lunch.'

He yelled back, 'Eat it yourself!'

Wednesday, 7 April
I hate Jeff today. He's making everything worse, just when it was getting better.

Chapter 15

I have been trying to get sick. I don't wear a sweater when I should, and two days ago I walked in the rain without my boots and my feet got soaked. But so far nothing has happened. Debbie once told me about a girl in her cabin at camp who liked to stay overnight in the infirmary. She used to rub the end of the thermometer until it went up to 102°. Then she'd stick it in her mouth and the nurse would think she was really sick.

This morning I tried doing that but it never went above 94° – and I rubbed it for ten whole minutes. So I held the tip of the thermometer next to the light bulb in my desk lamp and it went up to 105°. I figured I'd walk downstairs like that. Then my mother would take it out and wouldn't she be surprised when she saw what a high fever I had!

The only trouble was I didn't know the thermometer would be so hot. As soon as I put it into my mouth I burned my tongue something awful! I spit the thermometer out. It fell on the floor but it didn't break.

I will have to think up a better way to get my mother and father back together. I can't waste my time trying to get sick. That could take forever.

I had my piano lesson right before dinner tonight. Mrs Lennard told me to cut my nails shorter. She says she can hear a *click-click* sound when I play. And that from now on Mew can't sit on top of the piano when I take my lesson. I told her my cat is very musical and that she always sits on top of the piano when I practise. Actually, Mew is almost human, but I didn't say so.

Mrs Lennard looked at me kind of funny. I'll bet she wishes she was still teaching Jeff and not just me. It's no secret that he's the one with the talent. But this year he quit piano. I don't think I play so bad. It's just that my fingers don't always do what I want them to.

Before Mrs Lennard left she told me to practise the same songs for next week. She said I wasn't ready for anything new. I felt like asking her how she would play if her parents were getting divorced.

As soon as we sat down to dinner Amy said, 'Wendy, my friend in school, has a Talking Jessie Doll. She brought it in for Show and Tell. I want one too. The kind with the hair that grows.'

'Maybe for your birthday,' my mother said.

'My birthday's not until the end of June,' Amy told her.

'Well, that's not so far away,' Mom said.

84

'Oh, please, Mommy! I can't wait until my birthday!'

'I'm sorry, Amy. But you'll have to.'

'Why?' Amy asked.

'You know Mom doesn't have a lot of money to throw around,' I told Amy. 'Stop being so selfish.'

'I'll bet you Daddy would get it for me.'

'That's enough, Amy!' Mom shouted.

'I *hate* you.' Amy screamed. 'You made Daddy go away just so you could be mean to me!'

My mother reached across the table and smacked Amy. Then she sent her to her room.

'I thought you said there wouldn't be any more fighting once you and Daddy were apart,' I said.

Jeff laughed and got up from the table.

'Try to understand,' Mom told us. 'Won't you please try to understand?' She put her head down right on her plate and started to cry. She got gravy in her hair.

Thursday, 15 April
Sometimes I feel sorry for my mother and other times I hate her. And besides all that, I didn't laugh once today!

Chapter 16

Gary Owens wrote our class a letter. Mrs Singer found it in her mailbox in the office. It said:

Dear Mrs Singer and Class 6–108,
Texas is neat. It's warm enough to play baseball
even in the winter. We got a dog. His name is
Alexander, like the Great. We call him Al for short.
Most of the kids here are okay except for a few.
They call me the new kid. Here's my address in case
anybody feels like writing.
Gary Owens
16 Sanders Road
Houston, Texas

Mrs Singer said we should all write to Gary and that would be our English lesson for the day. I wrote:

Dear Gary,
It must be nice to be where it's warm. We made
Viking dioramas. Did you learn about the Vikings
yet? Your dog Al sounds very nice. I still have my
cat Mew, but I like dogs too. By now you're
probably not the new kid any more. Well, that's all
the news from here.

Your friend,
Karen Newman
(I hope you remember me!)

Mrs Singer made me copy my letter over because I didn't make paragraphs. There are a lot of things I would have told Gary, if only he had liked me before he moved away.

Chapter 17

My mother got a job! She's going to be the receptionist at the Global Insurance Company in East Orange. She'll probably get to bring home a million Day Books next year. She says this is just a stepping stone – something to get her going until she decides what kind of work she wants to do permanently.

Aunt Ruth and Uncle Dan came over tonight. My mother was in the basement working on an old trunk she picked up at some sale. She's refinishing it and lining the inside with flowered material. It's going to be for Amy's toys, she says. So Aunt Ruth and Uncle Dan went downstairs to see her. So did I. I wanted to hear what my mother had to say because I am almost positive Aunt Ruth doesn't want her to go to work.

'The children need you at home, Ellie,' Aunt Ruth said.

'They're in school all day,' Mom told her. 'They won't even know I'm gone. I'm only working from nine to three and Karen will watch Amy until I get home.'

'Except Wednesdays,' I reminded her. 'Don't forget I have Girl Scouts on Wednesdays.'

'Amy can play at Roger's for half an hour on Wednesdays. I'll be home by three thirty.'

'Suppose one of them gets sick?' Aunt Ruth asked. 'Then what?'

'Mrs Hedley can come. I'll make some kind of arrangement with her. Besides, they don't get sick that often.'

Isn't that the truth? And I've been trying so hard.

'Ellie . . .' Uncle Dan said. 'I wish you'd think this over for a while. Are you sure you can handle the responsibility of running a house and keeping a job?'

'Not to mention the children,' Aunt Ruth added.

'I think I can manage,' Mom said. 'At any rate, I'm going to give it a try.'

'What will people at work call you, Mom?' I asked. 'Will you be Mrs Newman or Miss Robinson, like before you were married?'

'I think I'll call myself Miss Newman. I'm used to being Ellie Newman. After all, that's who I've been for fifteen years.' Mom opened another can of shellac and started painting the trunk.

After Aunt Ruth and Uncle Dan went home I asked Mom, 'How come you didn't give in to Aunt Ruth this time?'

And Mom said, 'I don't always give in to Aunt Ruth.'

'Yes you do.'

'That isn't so, Karen.'

'Well I think it is. Every time you go shopping Aunt Ruth tells you what to buy. And when Amy had all those sore throats Aunt Ruth made you go to her doctor.'

'You're wrong,' Mom said. 'I may have listened to Aunt Ruth a lot of times but I don't always do what she thinks is right. And from now on I'm going to be much more careful to make up my own mind about everything.'

'Mom . . .'

'Yes?'

'What do you really want to do?'

'I don't know yet. But I'm going to try to find out.'

My mother is grown up. So how come she can't decide what she wants? Does she want to go to work or does she want to go to college? 'I sure hope you find out soon,' I told her.

'It has nothing to do with you, Karen. It isn't going to change your life one way or another.'

'That's what you say!'

'Look . . . some day you and Jeff and Amy will grow up and leave home. Then what will I have?'

'You see!' I raised my voice. 'That proves it! All you care about is yourself! You never think about me.'

'That's not so and you know it!' Mom said.

'Oh, yes, it is so! You never ask me what I think or what I feel or what I want . . . I wish I was never born!'

I ran upstairs, picked up Mew and took her to my room. I closed my door and put a chair up against it.

Pretty soon my mother knocked on the door and called me. I knew she would. 'Karen . . . this is silly. Let me in. I want to talk to you.'

'Go away,' I told her.

I'll bet anything that Mom will change her mind about her job just like she did about Daddy.

A few days after my mother started her job I had a dental appointment. Mom said from now on she will schedule our appointments later in the day, but just this once Aunt Ruth would pick me up at school and drive me to Dr Harrison's.

I am the only one in my family who has never had a cavity. I don't know if this is because I am a better tooth-brusher or because I was born that way. Whatever the reason, I'm glad.

Dr Harrison sings while he looks at your teeth. He has a terrible voice. He makes up his own words too. Usually they don't make much sense but they always rhyme. When he cleans my teeth I laugh. I can't stand that tickle on my gums. And when I laugh he tells me not to, because I open my mouth too wide.

91

Today he said that my teeth are in good shape and that I don't have to come back for another six months. But he gave me a fluoride treatment and I almost threw up. I hate fluoride treatments!

When I was through I told the nurse my mother would call to make my next appointment. Aunt Ruth put away her needlepoint and asked me if I would like to stop for a snack on the way home. I said, 'Sure.'

We went to Grunings on the hill. They have the world's most delicious ice cream. Aunt Ruth ordered a hot-fudge sundae with whipped cream and nuts. I guess she's off her diet this week. I ordered two scoops of coffee ice cream. I don't like sundaes. All that goo gets in the way and it makes you very thirsty.

When we were served and I took my first bite of ice cream I remembered that my teeth are very sensitive to cold and hot after a cleaning. The ice cream nearly killed me. I had to mash it all up and then lick it off the spoon so it wouldn't hurt my teeth.

'How are things going at home?' Aunt Ruth asked.

'Okay, I guess. Next week is Mom's and Dad's anniversary.'

'That's right,' Aunt Ruth said. 'I forgot all about it.'

'Are you sending a card?'

'No . . . when a couple is getting a divorce they don't want to be reminded of wedding anniversaries.'

I don't agree with that but I didn't tell Aunt Ruth. I think if we remind Mom and Dad about their anniversary they will feel very bad about getting a divorce. They will remember how happy they were when they first met and all that. Then they will see how silly it is of them not to get along. 'They'll be married sixteen years,' I told Aunt Ruth.

'That's right. I remember it very well because Mark had the chicken-pox and the wedding was at our house and your grandfather never had chicken-pox so the doctor gave him a shot. But two weeks later he got it anyway.'

'Garfa had chicken-pox?'

'All over him.' Aunt Ruth laughed a little. 'You know . . . I haven't thought about that in a long time. Sixteen years ago . . . Mark was just a little boy and now he's all grown up.'

'How long have you and Uncle Dan been married?' I asked.

'Twenty-six years.'

'That's really a long time!'

'Yes, it is.'

'Do you ever fight?'

'Sometimes.'

'But then you make up?'

'Either that or we forget about it.'

That's like me and my mother. We have just forgotten about the fight we had the other night. Neither one of us has mentioned it. Why couldn't she and Daddy have done that? 'You know something? I don't remember my parents fighting when I was little.'

'I suppose they got along better then,' Aunt Ruth said. 'It's only in the last six or seven years that things have been bad.'

'That long?' I couldn't believe it! How could two people not get along for so many years?

That night I was sitting in the den with Mew on my lap. Her fur shed all over my sweater. I got up to get her brush, then settled on the couch again. She doesn't always like me to brush her. Sometimes she gets mad and tries to bite the brush. Tonight she purred and let me do whatever I wanted.

Mom and Amy were watching TV. Jeff never sits with us any more, except at mealtime. Amy was snuggled up close to Mom, which is really unusual for her. She always used to do that with Daddy. When I am cuddling Mew I never feel bad that my mother or father is paying attention to someone else.

As I brushed Mew's fur I started to think about what Aunt Ruth had said – that my parents haven't got along for six or seven years. And that's when it hit me! If the trouble between Daddy and Mom started that long ago, maybe it had something to do with Amy. That would have been around the time she was born. Maybe they didn't plan to have her. Maybe they only wanted two kids – me and Jeff. But then when Amy was born, Daddy liked her best. Mom was angry that he picked a favourite and she got back at Daddy by making Jeff *her* favourite. So really, if Amy hadn't been born they'd still be very happy.

I wonder if Amy knows about that? Probably not. She is too young to figure out such a thing. If you ask me Val has it all wrong. I might be the middle child, but it looks like I am the only one who is normal. Amy and Jeff have the problems. Poor Amy! No wonder she can't sleep at night. I am lucky to be no one's favourite.

Chapter 18

On Friday night Mrs Hedley came and Mom went rushing off to her class at Seton Hall. When Mrs Hedley opened her knitting bag and pulled out a pile of yarn I left the room. Amy could help her make wool balls tonight! I had more important things to do.

I went up to the hideaway. The door was open. Jeff was lying on his bed with his eyes closed. Only his purple light was on. The whole room glowed.

'Hey Jeff . . .' I said.

'Yeah?'

'Did you remember that Monday is Mom's and Daddy's anniversary?'

'So?'

'Don't you think we should do something?'

'Are you kidding?'

'No . . . I think it would be very nice to have a little party or something.'

Jeff opened his eyes and sat up. 'They're getting divorced, Karen.'

'So?'

'So you don't go around giving parties for people who're getting divorced.'

'Don't you even want to sign my card?'

'You bought a card?' Jeff asked.

'Two,' I said, holding them up.

I bought them yesterday. One for Mom and one for Daddy. They are both the same. There's a picture of two bluebirds and it says *TO A SWELL COUPLE*. I'm going to mail them tomorrow morning because I want to make sure they are delivered on the twenty-sixth, and that's Monday. I'm sure when they remember that it is their six-teenth anniversary they will call their lawyers and cancel the divorce.

'Well,' I said to Jeff. 'You want to sign them or not?'

'You're nuts!' Jeff said. 'You can't send them anniversary cards like there's nothing wrong.'

'Says who?'

'You just can't.'

'Well, I'm going to. Amy's signing them and so am I and I think you should too.'

'That's the dumbest thing I ever heard.'

'This is your last chance to sign,' I told him.

'Forget it!'

'Okay, I will.' I turned and walked out of his room. Let him lie there forever – with his stupid purple light bulb!

When Amy came up to bed I showed her the cards. She liked them a lot. I told her she could sign them and she chose a different colour crayon for every letter in her name. And she didn't just sign *Amy* – she signed *Amy Denise Newman*.

On Saturday morning Mom said I could ask Debbie to sleep over if I wanted because she was going out to dinner with Aunt Ruth and Uncle Dan. 'I don't think we need Mrs Hedley any more,' Mom said. 'Jeff is old enough to be in charge.'

'I thought you said if we give up Mrs Hedley some other family will grab her.'

'They probably will,' Mom said. 'But it's foolish to pay her when we can manage by ourselves.'

Did Mr Hague tell Mom to watch her money? Or doesn't Daddy send enough for a baby-sitter?

Debbie came over in time for supper, which we made ourselves. We had hot dogs, potato chips and chocolate pudding for dessert. The only part of the night that wasn't fun was telling Amy that she couldn't sleep in my other bed. She cried and carried on but before Mom left she explained that Amy has her own room and that's where she has to sleep from now on. I don't think Amy ever told Mom that she is afraid we'll be gone in the morning. Maybe I should be the one to tell my mother. I don't know – Amy might not like it if I did. That is supposed to be our secret.

Mom got all dressed up and I couldn't help wondering if just Aunt Ruth and Uncle Dan were taking her to dinner or if maybe Henry Farnum was going along too. And I didn't want to ask her about it in front of Debbie anyway. Mom looked very nice and she smelled delicious. I think she was wearing the perfume Daddy gave to her last Christmas.

At ten o'clock Amy fell asleep in the den and Debbie and I carried her up to bed. We decided to leave her overhead light on all night. That way she might not get so scared if she woke up suddenly.

At quarter to eleven the phone rang. Debbie and I were in my room. I thought it might be Mom, checking to see how everything was. So I went into my mother's room and picked up the phone, but Jeff beat me to it on the kitchen extension. And it wasn't my mother either. It was Mary Louise Rumberger! I put one hand over the mouthpiece and called to Debbie, 'It's Mary Louise . . .'

Debbie came running. We shared the phone and listened. Imagine Mary Louise calling my brother at quarter to eleven at night! And they barely even talked. They just laughed very softly at each other.

I could hardly wait for Monday night. I hoped Daddy would call as soon as he saw his mail. Then he and Mom would talk about the day they got married sixteen years ago and they'd laugh about Garfa catching the chicken-pox!

Mom opened her mail as soon as she got home from work. I stood there watching her. After she read my card she did the craziest thing! She started to cry and she took me in her arms. She said, 'Oh, Karen . . .' over and over again.

Later Daddy called. Only he didn't call to talk to Mom like I was hoping. He called to talk to me. He said, 'Thanks, Karen . . . but from now on you have to remember we don't celebrate our anniversary any more. Try not to think of 26 April as a special day.'

Monday, 26 April
How can I not think about this day? It is special and it will always be special even if I am the only one who knows it!

Chapter 19

Jeff has a broken toe. He has to wear a sneaker with a big hole cut in it. His toe is bandaged and he pulls an athletic sock over that foot to keep the rest of his toes warm. He broke it himself. He dropped a weight on his foot. Dr Winters says he is lucky he didn't do more damage. He uses a cane to walk around. I wonder what Mary Louise Rumberger thinks of broken toes? She probably feels very sorry for him. She calls him every single night now.

Jeff doesn't talk to any of us. Not to me or Amy or my mother. He is getting just like Petey Mansfield. They can turn themselves off like radios. I am starting to really hate him!

Val invited me to sleep over Saturday night. I asked my mother if I could go. She said, 'I don't even know her, Karen. How can I let you sleep there overnight?'

'Please, Mom! She's very nice. So is her mother.' That was funny because I really don't know Mrs Lewis. I've seen her twice. She says hello, but that's about it. She is the best-looking mother I have ever seen. 'Daddy lives right upstairs,' I told Mom.

'You'll have to call him and see what he thinks,' Mom said.

'Now?'

'Yes, now.'

I picked up the phone and dialled. 'Hello Daddy? This is Karen . . . I'm fine . . . They're okay too. Daddy, Val wants me to sleep over Saturday night . . . Yes, I'm dying to but Mom won't let me unless you say I can. Well, because she doesn't know Val or Mrs Lewis . . . Okay, I'll tell her you're going to be home. Thanks a lot, Daddy. I'll see you Saturday. 'Bye.'

After that my mother said I could go.

The next night my father called to invite Jeff and Amy to stay over at his apartment Saturday night. Amy said she couldn't wait, but Jeff told Daddy he already made other plans. I'll bet they have something to do with Mary Louise.

On Saturday, before I left for Val's, I made my mother promise to take good care of Mew and to feed her *canned* food in the morning. I think Mom would give Mew food from a box if she could get away with it.

I picked Mew up and kissed her goodbye. I am not allowed to kiss her. It has something to do with the possibility of her carrying germs. So I take her into the bathroom with me, lock the door and kiss her as much as I want to.

Later, when Daddy called for us, me and Amy

were waiting by the front door. As soon as we were in the car Amy said, 'Jeff doesn't like me any more.'

My father said, 'Oh?'

'And he doesn't like Karen either. He doesn't like anybody. He's so mean! He's almost as mean as Mommy. She won't get a Talking Jessie Doll. The kind with the hair that grows.'

'Your mother's not mean, Amy,' Daddy said.

'How do you know? You don't live at home.'

'Because I know your mother and if she doesn't think you should have a Talking Jessie Doll right now she must have a good reason.'

'She's always leaving us alone,' Amy said. 'That's mean, isn't it?'

'I can't believe she leaves you alone,' Daddy said.

'She doesn't,' I told him. 'We don't use Mrs Hedley any more, that's all. Jeff is in charge when Mom goes out.'

'That sounds reasonable to me,' Daddy said.

Amy sulked the rest of the way to Daddy's apartment.

Chapter 20

I rang Val's bell. She let me in. I got there in time to meet her mother's boyfriend, Seymour Chandler. He doesn't really look anything like a boyfriend. He looks more like a grandfather to me. His hair is silver and he's kind of fat. But Mrs Lewis looked beautiful. I wouldn't want to have a mother that good-looking. I'd spend all my time worrying about how I was going to turn out compared to her. Not that Val is ugly. She's okay. But she doesn't look like her mother.

Val introduced me to Mr Chandler. She said, 'Seymour, this is my friend Karen. Her father lives upstairs. He's getting a divorce.' Then Val told me, 'Seymour's divorced too.'

'That's right,' Seymour said. 'I am. Twice, as a matter of fact.' Then he laughed.

Twice! I never even thought about getting divorced more than once. That must *really* be awful!

'Well, girls . . . Seymour and I are leaving now. You have a nice time,' Mrs Lewis told us. She leaned close to Val and kissed her good night. I noticed that her lips didn't touch Val's face. It was an air-kiss. 'Go to sleep by eleven, Valerie.'

'I will, mother,' Val said. She closed the door

behind them and fastened the three extra locks on it.

It must feel funny to see your own mother go out on dates.

'Well . . .' Val said. 'What do you want to do?'

'I don't know. I usually watch TV on Saturday nights.'

'TV ruins your mind,' Val said. 'Let's wash our hair.'

'Mine's not dirty,' I said. 'I just washed it Monday night.'

'Oh, come on, Karen. It'll be fun. Then we can soak in my mother's bubble bath. I always do that on Saturdays. Tell you what . . . I'll wash your hair first, then you can do mine.'

We went into the bathroom, where Val attached a rubber hose to the sink. 'It's like a beauty parlour. You'll enjoy it,' she said.

'Well . . . okay.'

Val fixed up a chair for me and spread a towel under my neck so it wouldn't hurt from leaning back so far. Then she went to work. I have never had such a good shampoo in my life. When I do it myself I don't get out all the soap, because my hair is so thick. But Val got it squeaky clean. She even gave me a cream rinse so I wouldn't get tangles. When that was done she wrapped my head in a big green towel.

Then it was my turn to do Val. I didn't do as

good a job on her. I tried, but her hair is awfully long. She had to give me advice. She said, 'Rinse behind my ears now. That's it. Watch it, Karen . . . the water's running down my face. Okay . . . now the cream rinse. Take two capfuls and rub it in all over. Good . . . rub some more in if that's not enough. Okay . . . now give me another rinse. Careful . . . it's going down my back.'

Val wrapped her head in a towel like mine, then she ran the tub. She poured in three-quarters of a bottle of bubble bath. While the tub was filling we rubbed each other's heads until they were damp. Val gave me a couple of barrettes to pin up my hair so it wouldn't get all wet when I took my bath.

She let the water run almost to the top of the tub and by then the bubbles were so thick you couldn't see through them.

I don't feel funny getting undressed in front of Debbie, because I have known her forever. But I did feel strange in front of Val. She could tell too. She said, 'If you want, I won't look until you're in the tub. You can hide under all the bubbles.' Then she turned around and I took off my clothes, dropped them in a heap on the floor and stepped into the tub. When I did, some of the water ran over the side.

Then Val got undressed and I didn't look, even though she didn't care if I did. More suds overflowed when she got into the tub, but Val didn't pay any attention to that. She said, 'When I grow up I'm going to be a nudist. People would get along better if they didn't wear any clothes. Then they couldn't pretend to be what they're not.'

'But you'd get cold in the winter,' I told her.

'Possibly. Maybe I'll move to a warmer climate.'

That reminded me of Gary Owens. I wonder if there are nudists in Houston?

We soaked in the tub for half an hour. Neither one of us used soap or a washcloth. I guess if you sit in bubble bath all that time you're bound to get clean.

When we finally came out of the tub Val put on her mother's terry robe, which was about four inches too long. It dragged all over the wet bathroom floor. I got into my pyjamas. We both smelled very nice. Then we brushed out each other's hair.

When that was done Val sat down on the closed toilet seat and rubbed some kind of oil all over her legs. 'I have to shave my legs now,' she said.

I don't know anybody who shaves her legs yet. Debbie says she will when she's fourteen or when her legs get hairy, whichever comes first.

Val ran a silver razor over her legs. *Zip zip zip.* She reminded me of my father, shaving his face. I used to love to watch him. He'd always put a dab of shaving cream on my nose when I was little. 'Don't you ever cut yourself?' I asked Val.

'Oh, sure. But nothing serious. I've had lots of practice. I've been shaving since September.'

'Did your mother show you how?'

'Nope. I learned myself. Want me to do yours?'

'No,' I said. 'My mother would kill me. She says the earlier you shave the more you have to keep shaving. And anyway, the hair on my legs is very light. See . . .' I held a leg up for Val to look at.

'You're lucky,' she said, inspecting it. 'I'm a very hairy person.'

I noticed that when we were in the tub but I didn't tell Val.

When she was done shaving I helped her clean up the bathroom. She took big handfuls of the suds that were left in the tub and threw them into the toilet. They made a sizzling sound. And even after she flushed three times there were still suds floating around. 'I think I used a little too much bubble bath tonight,' Val said. By then it was almost ten o'clock.

We went into Val's room. She has a trundle bed. It looks like just one bed, but underneath there's another one. It was already pulled out for me. I asked Val where she got the rug that's shaped like a foot and she said she saw an ad for it in *The New York Times* and cut it out to show her mother. Then she got it for her birthday.

'I put my new sheets on your bed,' Val said. 'Do you like them?'

They were pink-and-orange striped. 'They're really nice,' I said.

'I thought you'd approve.' Val snuggled down under her covers.

I'll bet it's lonely for her to spend every Saturday night all by herself. And Mrs Lewis goes out during the week too. No wonder Val hopes Seymour will marry her mother. Then she won't be alone so much.

'Val . . .' I said.

'Yes?'

'I still don't understand why you don't see your father. Couldn't you take a trip to San Francisco?'

'No. I told you before . . . he doesn't care anything about me.'

'How can you say that?' I asked.

'Because it's true.'

'Did your mother tell you?'

'No. That's one thing she won't admit. She says he's just busy.'

'Then you don't know if he really wants to see you or not.'

'Oh, I know all right. I'll show you,' Val said, reaching under her bed. She came up with her divorce book. She opened it and said, 'Listen to this. "Fathers who live close by but do not visit—" '

I interrupted. 'But your father doesn't live close by. He lives in San Francisco.'

'Wait a minute,' Val said. 'I'm not done reading.' She started again. ' "Fathers who live close by but do not visit and fathers who live far away and hardly ever call or write either do not love their children at all, or they love them very little." ' She closed the book, with her finger marking her place, and looked at me.

'It really says that?'

'It does.'

'Do you believe it?'

'Of course I do. It's true. Why should I kid myself?' She opened the book again. 'It says right here, "There is something very wrong with an unloving parent. He deserves pity as well as anger." I've got along without him for three years. I'll get along without him forever! He was never interested in me anyway.'

'What does your mother say . . . besides the bad things?'

'That he married her because she was pretty and he wanted to show her off, like a new coat or something. He never really loved her, she says.'

'I think my parents loved each other when they got married. Their wedding pictures look so happy. But my mother says they were too young.'

'How old was she?' Val asked.

'Nineteen.'

'You should never get married that young,' Val said.

'I'm not getting married at all!' I told her.

'I am,' she said.

That surprised me. 'You are?'

'Yes. When I'm twenty-seven and I'm a successful scientist.'

'You're going to be a scientist?' I asked. 'I thought you were going to be a nudist.'

'One thing has nothing to do with the other. I'll be both.'

'What kind are you going to be? Scientist, I mean.'

'I'm not sure. But I'm going to discover something important. I'll be famous and my father will want everyone to know that I'm his daughter. I'll be very cool about the whole thing. I'll admit that we're related but I won't say anything else.'

'If you get married ... will you ever get divorced?'

'No. Never!'

'Me neither,' I said. 'You know something? I think if my father could see my mother now he'd move back in.'

'Forget it. It'll never work.'

'How do you know?' I asked. 'You never even saw my mother.'

'I'm telling you, Karen. Just forget it.'

'I don't see how you can be so sure,' I said. 'My father's very lonely.'

'But that doesn't mean he and your mother are going to get back together.'

'Well, I still don't see how it can hurt to try.'

'Go ahead,' Val said. 'Try . . . you'll see . . . you'll be the one who gets hurt.' She put out the light then. 'Good night, Karen,' she said.

'Good night, Val.' I'll bet she doesn't want my parents to get back together. Just because her father moved to San Francisco and never sees her. But I'm still sure it will work.

Chapter 21

When Daddy drove us home on Sunday afternoon he asked me to run into the house and get Jeff. 'I have something to tell all three of you,' he said.

Jeff was playing the piano. I heard the music before I opened the front door. He's been spending a lot of time practising lately. He writes his own songs. Most of them are in a minor key and sound sad. His newest one is called 'Mary Louise . . . Please.' Those are the only words. Please what? I wonder. But I wouldn't dream of asking him.

I went inside and said, 'Hey Jeff . . . Daddy's out in the car. He wants to talk to you.'

Jeff banged the piano with both hands before he got up and stomped out of the house. I followed him. We both got into the back seat of the car. Amy was up front with Daddy.

My father turned around to face me and Jeff. 'I'm leaving for Las Vegas a week from tomorrow,' he said. 'I'm staying with Garfa for about six weeks and while I'm there I'll get the divorce.'

'You're getting a Nevada divorce?' Jeff asked.

'Yes,' Daddy told him.

'But why?' I said. 'Why can't you just get it right here in New Jersey?'

'Because that would take a long time,' Daddy said. 'At least a year.'

'So?' I asked.

'Well, your mother and I want to get things settled now. This isn't easy for either one of us.'

What's the big hurry? I wondered. Why can't they wait? Why does Daddy have to go away for such a long time? Unless . . . unless there's some other woman that he wants to marry! Thinking about that makes me sick. But it is possible. One night last week I called Daddy and there wasn't any answer. Maybe he was out with her then, making plans! Or could Mom be the one who wants the divorce right away? Suppose she wants to marry Henry Farnum! No, that can't be. We'd have met him by now. It's got to be Daddy! I wonder who the woman is? I hate her already. I will never speak to her. Not as long as I live!

That night I helped my mother do the dinner dishes. When we were almost through I said, 'Is Daddy getting married?'

Mom turned off the water and looked at me. 'Where did you ever get that idea?'

'Well, is he?'

'No,' Mom said.

'Are you positive?'

'Yes. The divorce has nothing to do with anyone else. You know that, Karen.'

'How can you be sure Daddy didn't meet somebody last week and now he wants to marry her?'

'I'm sure. That's all. Besides, he'd have told me.'

'Why should he tell you?'

'Just because. I know him. And he'd certainly tell you and Jeff and Amy. He wouldn't just run off and get married.'

'Then why is he in such a hurry to get the divorce?'

'Oh . . .' Mom said. 'So that's it!'

'Well?'

'He's going now because he can get away from the store now. In a few months he might not be able to.'

I thought that over. And I had to admit it makes sense. Maybe things aren't as bad as I thought.

Later I called Val. I said, 'If a person goes to Nevada for a divorce, can he change his mind about it at the last second and tell the judge to forget the whole thing?'

'Who's going to Nevada?' Val asked.

'Nobody special. But just suppose somebody did. Do you think the judge would understand and cancel the divorce?'

'I don't think anybody changes his mind at the last second.'

'But it's possible, isn't it?'

'Karen . . .' Val said.

'What?'

'I know your father's going to Las Vegas to get the divorce.'

'You do?'

'Yes. He told my mother the other day. We're going to take in his mail and newspapers while he's gone.'

'Oh.' No wonder Val tried to discourage me last night. She knew about Daddy all along.

'So why don't you just forget about him changing his mind?' Val said.

'Listen . . . when he gets out there and sees how much he misses all of us I'll bet you anything he *will* change his mind!'

'Don't count on it.'

'I've got to go now,' I said. 'I've got a ton of homework.'

I hung up the phone and went to my room. Mew was asleep on my bed. I lay down next to her and rubbed my face against her fur. 'I must do something, Mew,' I told her. 'I must do something right away to stop the divorce! There's only one week left.'

Chapter 22

I've got to get my mother and father into the same room. My new idea is this: I will ask Mrs Singer if I can bring my Viking diorama home now, instead of at the end of the month. It's in the showcase in the hall near our classroom. We have a whole Viking display. Everyone stops to look at it. Since my diorama is very fragile, Daddy will have to come into the house to see it. I wouldn't dare bring it out to the car or to his apartment. That's what I'll say anyway. He'll be very proud of me. I made a Viking ship with twelve small Vikings sitting in it. There are pink and purple mountains in the background and I used blue sparkle for the water. Even Mrs Singer said I did an excellent job. I'm glad she noticed.

Once Daddy comes home and sees Mom, everything will work out fine. I just know it. First they'll look at each other and then they'll touch hands. Finally Daddy will kiss her and they'll never fight again. Daddy will call Garfa to cancel his trip to Las Vegas and I will write to tell him how I got them back together. Garfa will write that he knew I'd be able to do it all along. And won't Val be surprised! I'll never tell my parents I planned the whole thing. Let them think it was all an accident.

On Monday morning I went up to Mrs Singer's desk and said, 'I'd like to bring my Viking diorama home this week.'

'But Karen,' Mrs Singer said, 'it's in the showcase.'

'I know,' I told her. 'But I have to take it home. So maybe we could put something else in the showcase.'

'Like what?' Mrs Singer asked.

'Oh, I don't know. A picture or a book. Anything.'

'I'd rather that you wait until the end of the month when we change the showcase.'

'I can't, Mrs Singer,' I said, raising my voice. 'I need it now!'

'What for?'

'For . . . for . . .' But I couldn't tell Mrs Singer why I needed it, even though I felt like yelling, 'To keep my parents from getting divorced.'

Instead I turned around and walked to my desk. As soon as I sat down Debbie leaned over and whispered, 'What's wrong?'

I made a face and shook my head towards Mrs Singer. Then my nose started to run and I knew I was going to cry. So I ran out of the room. I stood in the hall with my forehead pressed against the showcase window. My Viking diorama was in the corner, with a little sign under it that said *Made by Karen Newman*.

Debbie came out into the hallway. 'Are you okay?' she asked.

'I guess.'

'Mrs Singer said I should take you to the nurse's office.'

'I don't need any nurse,' I told her. We walked back to our classroom together.

I got through the rest of the day without doing any work. I made some plans though. If I could find the key to the showcase I could open it and take my diorama. That's not stealing. After all, it does belong to me! Mrs Singer keeps the key to the showcase somewhere in her desk. I'm sure of that.

At two thirty I excused myself to go to the girls' room. I wanted to get a good look at the showcase lock. Maybe I could pick it open with a bobby pin. But when I looked in the window I saw a big book with a Viking on the cover in the corner where my diorama used to be. I ran back into the classroom and told Mrs Singer, 'It's gone! My diorama is gone. Somebody stole it!'

Everybody in the room started to talk at once, but I didn't care. Mrs Singer shouted, 'Calm down! No talking at all!' Then she reached into her bottom desk drawer and pulled out my diorama.

'Nothing's happened to it, Karen. I took it out of the showcase myself. If it's that important to you, take it home.'

I didn't say anything. I couldn't. I just nodded and took the diorama to my desk. I guess even witches have good days!

Monday, 3 May
I am counting the seconds until Sunday when Daddy calls for us and I get him inside to see my diorama.

Chapter 23

My mother, Jeff, Amy and me are getting to be regulars at Howard Johnson's on the highway. We go there every Friday night because of Mom's English literature course.

The Howard Johnson's hostess knows us by now. She tries to give us the same booth every week. My mother likes it because it's not near the kitchen and it's away from the front door. Jeff has to sit on the aisle so he can stick out his foot. Next week the bandage is coming off his toe. If you ask me he likes his cane. It gets him a lot of attention.

Amy and I always order the same supper – hamburgers and french fries. We drink Ho-Jo Cola too. I think that's really Coke, even though the waitress won't admit it. Tonight Jeff ordered fried shrimp.

'You never eat fried shrimp,' my mother said.

'So I'll try it and maybe I'll like it,' he told her.

'I don't think this is the place to try something like that.'

'I feel like fried shrimp!' Jeff said. 'So I ordered it. So now forget about it!'

'Okay,' Mom said. 'It's just that you'll have to eat them whether you like them or not.'

'I said I'll eat them, didn't I?'

'I just want you to be sure.'

'Daddy always takes us out for steak,' Amy said.

'Daddy can afford to,' Mom told her.

This is the first time my mother has ever said anything like that. She looked at Jeff. 'Would you go wash up, please. Your hands are filthy.'

'I washed at home,' Jeff said.

'I'm asking you to go to the men's room and wash again.'

Jeff stood up, grabbed his cane and left the table. When he came back our main course was served. He sat down, picked up one shrimp and nibbled at it. 'Will you quit looking at me,' he said to me and Amy.

I didn't look at anything but my hamburger for the rest of the meal.

When my mother finished her dinner she said, 'Well, Jeff . . . how are they?'

'Not great,' he said. 'I didn't know they'd be all breaded like this.'

'I told you,' Mom said.

'Oh, lay off, will you!'

'Jeffrey . . .' Mom began.

But Jeff stood up then.

'Sit down,' Mom told him.

'No.'

'I said sit down!'

'No. I said *no*. Are you deaf or something?'

A lot of people were looking at us and my

mother was embarrassed. So was I. I hoped we wouldn't see anybody we knew.

Jeff took his cane off the coat hook and walked to the front of the restaurant.

'Where's he going?' Amy asked.

'Out to the car,' Mom said.

'How do you know?' Amy asked.

'Where else would he go?' Mom said.

'You want me to go see?' I asked.

'No,' Mom said. 'We'll have our dessert and when we're through we'll go to the car. Jeff's not going to spoil our dinner.'

We all had ice cream. When we finished my mother gave me the check and the money to pay the cashier while she took Amy to the ladies' room.

But when we went outside to the car Jeff wasn't there.

'Karen . . . check inside the restaurant again. He must be in there somewhere. Look in the men's room too.'

'Me?' I said. 'Me . . . go into the men's room?'

'Just knock on the door and ask if anybody saw Jeff.'

'Okay,' I said. I went back inside. I checked the counter. He wasn't there. I walked all through the restaurant, pretending I had left something in our booth. I didn't see Jeff anywhere. So I stood in front of the men's room. I didn't knock like my mother told me to do. I couldn't. Suppose somebody came to the door and when they opened it I saw inside? No, I didn't want to look inside the men's room. Even though I've always wondered what it's like in there. Tonight wasn't the right time to find out.

'You want something?' a man asked me.

'No,' I said.

'Then, excuse me, please. I'm trying to get in here.'

'Oh,' I said, jumping away from the door. 'Would you do me a favour?'

'Sure,' he said. 'What is it?'

'Would you see if my brother's in there?'

'What's he look like?'

'He's fourteen and he's got a broken toe.'

'All right. Just a minute,' the man said.

He went inside. I turned my back to the door. He came right away. 'Nobody's in here,' he told me.

'Well, thank you anyway,' I said.

I went back outside and told my mother that Jeff wasn't anywhere in Howard Johnson's, including the men's room. 'Maybe he went home,' I said.

'No. You can't walk from here,' my mother told me. 'There's no way.'

'Well, then, where is he?' I said.

'I don't know,' Mom answered. 'Now stop

asking me questions and give me a minute to think.'

'The one who asks the most questions learns the most,' Amy said.

'Oh, shut up,' I whispered.

'Why don't you?'

After a minute my mother said, 'We'll drive home now. Then I'll decide what to do. I can't think here.'

When we got home Mom waited until nine o'clock before she did anything. Then she called Aunt Ruth and Uncle Dan. They came right over. Uncle Dan said the first thing to do was to call the police. But my mother didn't want to. So Uncle Dan said, 'Okay . . . but that's what I'd do if he was my son.'

Mom said, 'Let's try the hospitals first.'

So Uncle Dan sat down by the phone in the kitchen and called all the local hospitals. Jeff wasn't in any of them. I guess my mother thought Jeff got run over or something. Otherwise I don't know why she wanted Uncle Dan to call the hospitals.

Aunt Ruth said we should try his friends. So my mother asked me to make a list of all the kids Jeff might go to see. I couldn't decide whose name to put first – Petey Mansfield or Mary Louise Rumberger. I decided that Jeff, being in such a bad mood, would pick Petey. I handed Uncle Dan a list of twelve names. He called every one but none of them had seen Jeff.

'He could be at Bill's,' Uncle Dan said.

'No. How could he have got there?' my mother asked.

'Maybe he hitched,' I said.

'He knows I don't like him to hitch rides,' Mom said.

Maybe he knows it, I thought, but he hitches all the time. I've seen him do it. All the big kids hitch after school.

'And Bill wouldn't have been at the apartment anyway,' Mom said. 'It's Friday night. The store's open late.'

'How about the store?' Aunt Ruth said. 'Maybe he went to see Bill there.'

'Want me to call?' I asked.

'No,' Mom said. 'I don't want Bill to find out about Jeff.' She checked her watch. 'Anyway, Bill must be home by now. The store closes at nine.'

'He's going to have to know, Ellie. He is the boy's father,' Uncle Dan said.

'Would you call him, Dan? I just can't,' Mom told him.

So Uncle Dan called my father and when he hung up he said that Daddy was on his way over.

Chapter 24

When my father got to our house I was hoping he would take Mom in his arms and kiss her and tell her not to worry, because everything was going to be all right. Instead he said, 'Did you call the police yet?'

And Mom said, 'Oh, Bill . . . do we have to? Why get Jeff mixed up with the police?'

'I suppose you have a better idea?' Daddy asked.

'No,' Mom said. 'I haven't any ideas at all.'

'I'm not surprised,' Daddy said.

Mom looked around. I think she wanted to throw something at Daddy. But there were too many people in the room. I saw Aunt Ruth raise her eyebrows at Uncle Dan.

My father walked into the kitchen and picked up the phone. He called the police. He told them his son was missing and gave them his name and our address. When he hung up he said, 'They'll be right over.'

We've never had a policeman in our house. The only time I've ever been close to one is on the street. Sergeant Tice got to our house in ten minutes. He was chewing gum and he had a pad and pencil with him, just like on TV. Aunt Ruth showed him into the living room, where we all sat down. He started asking questions right away.

'Name of the missing boy, please.'

'Jeffrey Peter Newman,' Daddy said. 'We call him Jeff.'

Sergeant Tice snapped his gum and wrote that down. 'Age?' he asked next.

'Fourteen,' my mother said. 'He'll be fifteen in August.'

Mew walked into the living room then. I called, 'Psst . . . psst . . .' and she came to me. She jumped up on my lap, made herself into a fur ball and started purring.

'Do you have a recent snapshot of him?' Sergeant Tice asked.

'I don't know,' my mother said. 'I think we might have one from last summer. Karen . . . would you see if you can find one?'

'I don't know where any pictures are,' I told her.

Sergeant Tice said, 'Never mind. Let's get a good description of the boy now. Later, if you can come up with a picture, fine.'

'Well, he's about five foot seven,' Daddy said. 'And he weighs about one-thirty-five.'

'Hair?' Sergeant Tice asked.

'Brown,' Mom said. 'Down to his collar in back and just over his ears in front.'

'What's he wearing?'

'Jeans, a grey sweatshirt and a navy jacket,' Mom said.

'Eyes?'

'They're blue,' I said.

'Complexion?'

'Fair,' Daddy said. 'And he's got a dimple in his chin.'

'And some zits on his face,' Amy added. 'They're pimples if you don't already know.'

My mother looked over at Amy then, as if remembering for the first time that she was in the room. 'Go up to bed now, Amy. It's after ten!'

'No,' Amy said.

'Ruth . . . would you take her up and get her into bed?' Mom said.

'No!' Amy yelled. 'I want to stay . . . I want to stay and listen.'

Aunt Ruth tried to pick up Amy but Amy kicked so hard Aunt Ruth couldn't get hold of her.

'Daddy . . .' Amy cried. 'Don't let her take me away. Daddy . . . help!'

That sister of mine can really be impossible. And if you ask me she was doing it on purpose! But Daddy went to her and held her in his arms and stroked her hair and said, 'It's all right, baby. Everything's going to be all right.'

She really acts like a spoiled brat when Daddy is around.

Sergeant Tice cleared his throat to get our attention again. 'Any idea where he might be headed?'

'None,' Mom said. 'We've tried his friends but nobody knows where he is.'

'Any reason you can think of for him running off?'

'He got mad at Mommy!' Amy said. 'Because he didn't like his fried shrimp!'

Sergeant Tice looked at my mother.

'We did have a few words,' she told him. 'He got angry and walked out of the restaurant. Howard Johnson's on the highway.'

Sergeant Tice wrote that down. 'Is he on drugs?'

Daddy said, 'Of course not!'

'Are you certain?' Sergeant Tice asked.

'Damn right I'm certain,' Daddy told him, but he was glaring at my mother.

Sergeant Tice closed his notebook and stood up. 'Well . . . these kids usually head for New York. We'll see what we can do.'

Mom stood up too. 'That's all?' she asked. 'You'll see? What are we supposed to do in the meantime?'

'Just carry on,' Sergeant Tice said. 'Not much else you can do. He'll probably show up. Most of them do.'

'He's walking with a cane,' I said. 'He's got a broken toe.' I could just picture Jeff on his way to New York. He'd fall down every few miles and

130

he'd be cold and hungry and nobody would help him. Maybe I'll never see him again.

'Well, he can't get very far like that,' Sergeant Tice said. 'I'll be in touch.'

We walked him to the front door. I saw him spit out his gum by our dogwood tree.

Aunt Ruth said she'd make some coffee and Uncle Dan excused himself to go to the bathroom. Daddy carried Amy upstairs and put her to bed. When he came back down he and Mom went into the living room.

Now that the police business is out of the way, they can have a chance to be alone, I thought. They'll see that they belong together. That we're a family. Any minute now Daddy will tell her he's sorry he left.

I stayed in the kitchen with Aunt Ruth and Uncle Dan. I guess they wanted to hear what was going to happen as much as I did.

The first thing Daddy said was, 'I want the truth and I want it now.'

'I have nothing to say to you,' Mom told him.

'You damn well better have something to say! Because I want to know why my son ran away!'

'Your son!' Mom shouted. 'He's my son too . . . and don't you forget it!'

'When I left this house he was fine,' Daddy said. 'But you fixed that, didn't you?'

It's not going to work, I thought. They're just like they were before, only worse.

Mom yelled, 'Did you ever stop to think maybe it was your fault Jeff ran off? You're not exactly a perfect father!'

'Shut up!' Daddy raised his voice too. 'You want everybody to hear us?'

'I don't give a damn who hears! You make me sick!' Mom yelled.

'I'm warning you, Ellie . . .'

'Lay a hand on me and I'll have you locked up,' Mom screamed.

Was he going to hit her?

'I wouldn't waste my time,' Daddy shouted.

No, he wasn't going to hit her.

'That's the trouble with you,' Mom hollered. 'You think everything is a waste of time . . . me, the kids, the house, everything! The only thing you care about is the store! That goddamned store is your whole life!'

'I never heard you complain when the store got you a new car or this house or a vacation,' Daddy yelled.

'Those aren't the only things in life.'

'Come off it, Ellie.'

'No, I won't! You never looked at me as a person. I have feelings . . . I have ideas . . . did you ever stop to think about that?'

Amy ran into the kitchen then. She was crying. Uncle Dan picked her up and held her to him.

'Now you listen to me,' Daddy shouted.

'No!' Mom hollered. 'I'm tired of listening to you.'

'And I'm still tired of the whole business. You don't know what you want. You never did. And you never will! Because you never grew up! You're still Ruth's baby!'

Aunt Ruth pressed her lips together so tight they disappeared.

My mother shouted, 'I should have listened to Ruth a long time ago. I should have listened the first time I brought you home. She saw you for what you are. Conceited, selfish—'

'One more word and I'm going to take the kids away from you!'

'Don't you dare threaten me!' Mom screamed.

'I mean it. So help me. I'll have you declared incompetent.'

'You rotten bastard . . .'

There was an awful crash in the living room then and I ran in to see what happened. One of Mom's best china babies was on the floor, smashed, like the mocha-icing cake.

'That's how you settle all your problems, isn't it?' Daddy said with a terrible laugh. 'Just like a two-year-old.'

Mom started to cry. She bent down and tried

to pick up the pieces of her antique. I think it was the first time she ever broke anything she loved.

Then Daddy backed up and sat down on the chair by the fireplace, right on top of Mew. Mew howled and Daddy jumped. 'Damn cat!'

I shouted, 'You never liked her, did you?' I could see that Daddy thought I was talking about Mom, but really I meant Mew.

I don't know what they started yelling about then but I couldn't stand it any more so I put my hands over my ears and I started to scream. And I screamed and I screamed and I screamed, without stopping to take a breath. I saw Aunt Ruth and Uncle Dan and Amy and my mother and my father, just standing there like idiots, watching me scream, but still I didn't stop. I kept on screaming . . . until Daddy slapped me across the face.

And then I cried.

Chapter 25

When I opened my eyes it was morning. The first thing I saw was my Viking diorama sitting on top of the dresser. The sunlight coming through my window hit the blue sparkles and made them shine. I threw off my covers and jumped out of bed. I grabbed the diorama and flung it against the wall. It didn't break. Two of the Vikings fell out of their ship but the box was okay. So I stamped on it with both feet until there was nothing left but a broken shoebox and a lot of blue sparkle all over my rug. Then I kicked it as hard as I could, again and again. *Stupid, ugly Viking diorama! I hate you!*

I got back into bed and pulled the covers over my head. I was all set to cry, but the tears didn't come this time.

I must have been a crazy person to think that my silly diorama could work magic. Now I know the truth. My parents are not going to get back together. And there isn't one single thing I can do about it! My mother doesn't think Daddy is a wonderful person. She was feeding me a bunch of lies. Val was right. Not that Daddy thinks much of Mom either. Well, I'm through fooling myself.

I rolled over. I wonder where Jeff is. I think he would have liked the way I screamed last night.

I'm sorry he missed it. I'll bet he wishes he had some of those fried shrimps with him, breaded or not. He must be hungry by now. I hope he's okay. I don't want anything bad to happen to him, even though I did hate him for a while. If he doesn't come home Daddy won't be able to go to Las Vegas on Monday. Hey, I'll bet that's why Jeff picked last night to run away! Maybe he knew what he was doing after all. Except for one thing. He didn't hear them fighting so he doesn't know that they're hopeless. Poor Jeff! He ran away for nothing.

The phone rang, but I didn't jump up to answer it as usual. My mother came into my room. I closed my eyes and pretended to be asleep.

'Karen . . . are you awake?' Mom asked.

I didn't answer her.

She stood next to me and shook my shoulder a little. 'Karen, your father wants to talk to you.'

This is the first time she's ever called him my *father*. I still didn't answer.

'Karen . . . are you okay?'

I could tell by her voice she was getting upset because I wouldn't open my eyes. So I got out of bed on the side away from where Mom was standing and I said, 'I'm up and fine.' I walked from my room, across the hall, to hers. I picked up the phone. 'Hello.'

'Karen, about last night . . .' Daddy began.

'I don't want to talk about it,' I told him.

So Daddy said, 'Well, I want you to know it was just because we were so upset about Jeff.'

'Sure,' I said.

'And I don't want you to worry about your brother either. Because I've already hired a private detective and he'll certainly find him if the police can't.'

'That's good,' I said.

'Listen, Karen, the only reason I slapped you last night was because you were hysterical. And that's what you have to do when someone's hysterical.'

'That's okay,' I told him. I haven't ever been hysterical before. I wonder if I ever will be again?

'Are you still flying to Las Vegas on Monday?'

'I don't know yet,' Daddy said. 'It all depends on Jeff.'

'If he doesn't come home you're not going?'

'I'm not going anywhere till I know Jeff's okay. My trip can wait a week or two,' Daddy said. 'If you need me for anything I'll be at the store all day.'

'Okay. 'Bye.' I hung up and went back to my room. My mother was making my bed. She looked very tired. When she was done she sat on the edge of the bed and said, 'Karen, about last night . . .'

I told her the same thing I told Daddy. 'I don't want to talk about it.'

But she said, 'I think you should know that it was just because we were so worried about Jeff.'

'Sure,' I said. 'I know.'

'And we didn't really mean any of the things we said.'

'How about Daddy taking us away from you? Can he do that?'

'No, of course not. That was just his way of hurting me. I told you, we didn't mean anything we said last night.'

I didn't believe that. I think they really meant *all* the things they said to each other.

My mother blew her nose. When she was done she asked, 'What happened to your Viking diorama?'

'It broke,' I told her. 'But don't worry about the mess. I'll clean it up.'

'I wasn't even thinking about the mess. I just think it's a shame that it broke. It was beautiful.' Mom stood up and checked her watch. 'It's almost nine o'clock. I've got to run downtown to police headquarters. I found a picture of Jeff for Sergeant Tice.'

'Which one did you find?'

'His school picture,' Mom said, pulling it out of her pocket. She showed it to me.

'That's a nice one,' I said.

Mom nodded. 'Hurry and get dressed now, Karen. I want to go right away.'

'Why can't I stay here and watch Amy?'

'Amy's not home. Aunt Ruth picked her up early this morning.'

'Well, you go ahead and I'll stay here and clean up my room.'

'I don't want to leave you alone,' Mom said.

'But suppose Jeff calls and there's no answer. What will he think?'

'I never thought of that,' Mom said. 'You're right. You better stay here just in case. I won't be gone long.'

As soon as my mother left the house I went down to the kitchen. I was very thirsty. I felt like drinking a whole giant-sized can of pineapple juice. I gulped down two full glasses, then poured a third and walked into the living room. The smashed china baby was gone, but all the drawers in my mother's antique chest were halfway open and the floor was covered with photos. There were so many of them!

I put my glass on the coffee table, sat down on the floor and picked up a picture. It was of me when I was little. My two front teeth were missing. I was standing next to a huge fish and crying. I remember I was really scared. I thought the fish could bite me. I didn't know it was dead.

There was another picture that showed all of us at a picnic. I must have been about eight. That was the day Jeff's kite got caught in the tree and I fell into the brook.

I found our baby pictures. And one of Daddy and Mom at a costume party. My mother was wearing some dumb-looking Cleopatra wig. She and Daddy were laughing.

I grabbed up the photos and stuffed them back into the drawer. Then I ran upstairs to my room and took my cat bank off the dresser. Jeff gave it to me for my last birthday. He said he knew I'd rather keep my money in a cat than in a pig. I pulled the stopper out of the bottom of the bank and dumped all the money on to my bed. There was $10.49. Good! The divorce book costs $7.95, Val said. So I have enough.

I got dressed, threw my diorama into the garbage and took out the vacuum. There was no other way to get rid of the blue sparkle all over my rug.

When my mother got back from police headquarters I was still vacuuming.

'You didn't have to do that,' Mom said.

'I felt like it,' I told her. 'Did Sergeant Tice find out anything yet?'

'Not yet,' Mom said. 'But he will. Especially now that he has the picture. That should help a lot. Jeff might even be home this afternoon.'

'Sure,' I said.

'You know what I'm going to do?' Mom asked.

'No, what?'

'I'm going to give Jeff's room a good cleaning. The closets and everything.'

Why would she do a silly thing like that? Jeff likes his room messy. The messier the better.

Mom took the vacuum. 'I want his room to look really nice when he comes home. You want to help?' she asked me.

'I can't,' I said. 'I have to go over to the shopping centre. I need something for a school project.'

Mom acted like she hardly heard me. 'Be careful' was all she said.

The shopping centre isn't that far from our house. I rode my bike straight to the bookstore. I had the paper with Val's information on it tucked away in my pocketbook. I asked the saleslady for *The Boys and Girls Book About Divorce* by Richard A. Gardner, MD, published by Science House, Inc, illustrated by Alfred Lowenheim, with a foreword by Louise Bates Ames.

She seemed pretty impressed that I knew so much about it. She smiled at me a lot. Then she said, 'I'm sorry, but we don't have that book in stock. We'll have to order it for you.'

Imagine not having such an important book in stock! What is the matter with this bookstore? I asked her how long it would take to get it and she told me *maybe two weeks*. I said I didn't think I could wait that long and she smiled again and told me she'd put a rush on it and it might come through sooner. I had to pay in advance and write down my name, address and phone number. I don't know how I am going to last two whole weeks without that book!

Chapter 26

Dear Garfa

How are you? I hope you're fine. Yesterday I ordered The Boys and Girls Book About Divorce. *Did you ever hear of it? It's a very famous book and I need it a lot. I need it because Daddy and Mom are definitely going to get divorced! I've tried hard to get them back together. Honest! But nothing works. I have discovered something important about my mother and father. When they are apart they're not so bad, but together they are impossible!*

Anyway, I hope you understand and won't be too disappointed, even if this is the first divorce in the history of the Newman family. Do you want to hear something funny? When Daddy told us he was flying to Las Vegas to get the divorce I still didn't believe it would really happen. Now I believe it! Another thing I think you should know is this – I don't look like Grandmother Newman at all. I just pretended to agree with you. I don't look like anyone but ME! I hope Mattie is fine and that you are having fun.

Love,
Karen

Maybe I should have mentioned something about Jeff in my letter but I think that would upset Garfa even more. And I am hoping that by the time my letter gets to Las Vegas Jeff will be home.

I folded the letter, put it in its envelope and licked it closed. I had to sneak an airmail stamp out of my mother's desk. I didn't want to ask for one because then I would have to explain why I was writing to Garfa. After breakfast I walked down to the corner and dropped the letter in the mailbox.

My mother spent all of Sunday morning washing and ironing Jeff's shirts. If you ask me she was just keeping busy so she wouldn't have to think about all the awful things that might happen to him.

That afternoon Aunt Ruth and Uncle Dan brought Amy home. Then we all sat around in the living room, waiting for something to happen. But nothing did. Uncle Dan called my father a couple of times. Daddy didn't want to leave his apartment in case Jeff decided to go there. Mom called police headquarters once, but Sergeant Tice wasn't in and there weren't any messages for my mother. It was a very gloomy afternoon.

At three thirty the phone rang and I jumped up to answer it.

'Hello, this is Mary Louise Rumberger calling. Is Jeff home?'

At first I didn't answer her. I didn't know what to say.

'Hello . . .' she said again. 'Is anyone there?'

'Yes,' I told her. 'I'm here.'

'May I please speak to Jeff?'

'No . . . he's not in right now,' I said. 'Can I take a message?'

'Who is this?' she asked.

'It's Karen . . . his sister.'

'Oh. Well, tell him I called and ask him to call me back.'

'Okay . . . I'll tell him.'

'What time do you think he'll be home?'

'I don't know,' I said. 'Maybe around five or five thirty.' I don't know why I said that.

'Okay. Thank you,' Mary Louise said.

'You're welcome.' I hung up the phone and went back into the living room. 'That was Mary Louise Rumberger,' I said. 'She wanted to talk to Jeff.'

'I hope you didn't tell her anything,' Mom said.

'I just told her he wasn't home right now.'

'That was very good thinking, Karen,' Aunt Ruth said.

'Is it a secret that Jeff is lost?' Amy asked.

'Kind of,' Uncle Dan said. 'Can you keep a family secret?'

'I guess so,' Amy said.

★

An hour later Aunt Ruth ordered some pizzas for supper and I went outside to wait for the delivery truck. It was a good excuse to get away from everybody.

I sat down on our front steps. Mew ran out of the bushes and rubbed up against me. I picked her up. Her front paws smelled like mouse. Mew loves springtime. She sleeps a lot during the day and prowls around at night. The Great Grey Hunter, I call her. She brings a mouse or a mole to our door every morning. This doesn't make my mother happy. And to tell the truth, I don't like to be the one to get the shovel and scoop up Mew's catch. I love her a lot and I'm glad she's happy, but I wish she wouldn't bring home so many surprises.

In a little while I saw a girl walking up the street. When she got to our house she turned and came up the driveway. It was Mary Louise Rumberger. I knew it right away. And if I hadn't recognized her face I'd have known her by the Noxzema smell.

She said, 'Hi. I'm Mary Louise.'

I said, 'I know. I'm Karen.'

Then we just looked at each other until Mary Louise said, 'I brought Jeff a book he wants to read.'

'Oh, that's nice,' I said. 'You can leave it with me and I'll give it to him.'

'I'd rather give it to him myself.'

'Jeff isn't here right now,' I said.

'Where is he?' Mary Louise asked.

I knew she'd say that sooner or later. 'He's not home,' I told her.

'I know,' she said. 'You already mentioned that.'

This conversation might last forever, I thought. I'll keep telling her Jeff isn't here and she'll keep saying she knows.

'Well, where is he?' Mary Louise asked again.

'Who?'

'Jeff!'

'Oh, Jeff. He should be back soon.'

'Do you know that somebody called my house Friday night looking for him?'

'Yes,' I said. 'That was my uncle.'

'Why did he call my house? Didn't he know where Jeff was?'

'I guess he thought Jeff was with you. But really he was in New York visiting his friend from camp.' There, that sounded pretty good.

'None of this makes any sense to me,' Mary Louise said.

'It does, if you really think about it,' I told her.

'I didn't know Jeff was going to visit his friend from camp.'

'He doesn't tell you everything, does he?'

'I don't know,' Mary Louise said. 'I thought he would have mentioned something like that. He was supposed to meet me at the Y Saturday night.'

'Oh, well probably he didn't mention it because it was a last-minute thing. He didn't plan to go. He just went.'

'Why didn't you tell me that when I called?'

'I don't know,' I said. 'I guess I forgot.'

'How long will Jeff be gone?' Mary Louise asked.

'Oh, he'll be back any day now.'

'You mean you don't know *exactly* when?'

'Sure I do,' I told her. 'Any day. Soon. This week, I think!' I was getting in deeper and deeper.

Mary Louise shook her head. 'I'm having a party Friday night. Jeff is supposed to be there. If he's not coming back I'm going to cancel my party. Why should I have a party without him?'

'I don't know,' I said. I wished she would stop sniffling like that. I didn't want her to cry.

'You can tell him for me that if he doesn't come home by Friday I never want to see him again!' Mary Louise started down the front walk, holding her book tight against her.

'Hey, Mary Louise . . .' I called.

She turned around. 'What?'

'I think he'll come back for your party.'

'I hope you're right,' she said as she walked away.

I hoped so too.

Sunday, 9 May
I am so afraid J.N. is dead!

148

Chapter 27

Mom didn't go to work on Monday and when I got home from school I found her sound asleep on the living-room couch. I called Aunt Ruth. 'Did you hear anything about Jeff?' I asked.

'No, not a thing.'

'Mom is sleeping. Should I just leave her alone?'

'Yes,' Aunt Ruth said. 'I finally got her to take one of the sleeping pills the doctor prescribed. You know she hasn't slept since Friday.'

'I know it,' I said. 'I can take care of Amy when she comes home. So don't worry.'

'Thanks, Karen. I'll be over with something for supper about five o'clock.'

'Okay. 'Bye.'

I got a blanket from upstairs and covered my mother. I'm worried about her. If anything happens to Mom what will become of me and Amy?

Where is that detective my father hired? And how about Sergeant Tice? What is he doing besides chewing his gum?

I've got to try to find Jeff myself.

On Tuesday I went to the Mansfields' after school. I had to start somewhere and Petey was number one on my list. Brian answered the door.

'Hey, Karen,' Brian said. 'What are you doing here?'

'I came to see Petey,' I told him. 'Is he home yet?'

'Yeah, he's upstairs. What do you want to see him for?'

'It's personal,' I said.

'Oh, yeah?' He started to laugh. 'How personal?'

'Look, Brian, just tell Petey I'm here, will you?'

Brian turned away from me and yelled up the stairs. 'Hey, Petey . . . somebody's here to see you about something personal.'

'Very funny,' I told Brian.

'Yeah . . . I'm a riot . . . everybody knows that!'

I wonder if it's true that Brian likes me?

Petey came running down the stairs, but when he saw me he stopped.

'Could I see you alone?' I asked him. 'Outside maybe?'

Brian made a noise then. It sounded like *woohoo!*

Petey nodded at me and we both walked outside. He even shut the front door in Brian's face so he wouldn't be able to hear anything.

'Listen, Petey,' I said. 'If you know anything about my brother you better tell me. Because my mother's really sick about him. I mean it . . . she's sick! And if he's dead . . . if Jeff is dead . . . I want to know it! And I want to know it now!' I put my hands on my hips and waited.

Petey did the craziest thing then. He started to laugh. And that got me mad! 'I don't see anything funny,' I said. 'Maybe you think it's funny that my brother could be dead in some alley, but I don't!'

Petey just kept laughing.

'Do you understand me, Petey? Please tell me if you at least understand what I'm saying.'

Petey stopped. 'Jeff's not dead,' he said in this deep voice that surprised me. So he can talk!

'How do you know he's not dead?' I asked.

'I just do, that's all.'

'You tell me where he is, Petey Mansfield!'

'I don't know.'

'Then you don't know if he's dead either, do you?'

'I'm telling you, Karen, he's not dead! Now that's all I'm going to say!'

'Well, if you know that then you know where he is and you can just tell him for me that if my mother has a heart attack or something, it's all his fault. You hear that, Petey? It's all his fault! You just tell him that for me. And if you're lying about Jeff being dead and anything happens to my mother, then it's all *your* fault!'

'You're really something, Karen. You know that? You're really something!' Petey said.

I took a good look at him. Maybe he's not so bad. Maybe if he was the last boy on earth I would marry him. That is, if I was going to get married at all, which I am not.

I went home. I wanted to tell Mom not to worry, that Jeff wasn't dead. But I had no proof. So I didn't say anything.

Later that night, after Amy was in bed, I went into the kitchen to get an apple. While I was peeling it the phone rang. I answered. It was Jeff! He said, 'Hello, Karen.' Just like that. When I've been worrying he might be dead! *Hello, Karen.* Like there was nothing wrong at all. I hollered, 'MOM . . .' and dropped the phone.

'What is it, Karen? What's wrong?' Mom asked.

'It's Jeff,' I said. 'On the phone.'

'Oh, thank God!' Mom said. She picked up the phone. 'Jeff. Jeff, where are you? Are you all right? Oh, Jeff, please come home . . . yes . . . yes, no questions. I don't care where you've been as long as you come home. Where are you now? Jeff . . . Jeff . . .'

My mother put the receiver back on the hook. 'He hung up,' she said. 'I don't know where he is, but he's coming home.'

'When, Mom? Did he say?'

'I don't know. Tonight I think. Karen . . . you go up to bed now.'

'Oh, Mom.'

'Please, Karen! I don't want Jeff to have to face anyone but me tonight. You'll see him tomorrow . . . or whenever he's ready to see you. Okay?'

'Okay . . . if you say so.'

As I went upstairs I heard Mom phone Aunt Ruth. 'Jeff's okay,' she told her. 'He's coming home . . . Oh, Ruth, I can't . . . You call Bill for me.'

I went to my room, took out my Day Book and wrote:

Tuesday, 11 May
J.N. is alive! I heard his voice. He is coming home.
M.L.R. doesn't have to worry. He'll be able to go to her party.

I didn't get into bed. I turned out my light and sat in front of the window. I waited and waited. Finally I saw Jeff come up the walk.

Maybe Petey did know where Jeff was. Maybe he told him to come home. I wouldn't be surprised if that's what happened. Or maybe Petey didn't know a thing. I suppose that's possible too. Jeff could have decided to come home all by himself. I'll probably never know the truth.

I sneaked out into the upstairs hall. With the lights turned off nobody could see me, but I could see down. My mother hugged Jeff for a long time. Then she held him away to get a good look at him. While she was looking he started to cry. Just like a little kid. Imagine Jeff acting like that! They sat down on the bottom step then and my mother held him tight. I always knew she loved him best.

Chapter 28

'Jeff is back!' my mother told me and Amy at breakfast the next morning. 'I'm taking the day off from work.'

'Where is he?' Amy asked.

'In his room . . . asleep,' Mom said.

'Where was he?' Amy asked.

'Wherever he was he's home now. And that's what counts. We aren't going to ask him any questions. I want you both to understand that completely.'

'The one who asks the most questions—' Amy started to say.

But my mother didn't let her finish. 'Never mind about that. No questions!'

'Okay,' Amy said. 'You don't have to yell.'

'I'm not yelling,' Mom told her.

Amy fiddled around with her waffles. We eat them every morning now. They're the frozen kind that you pop in the toaster. I think they're good. We never had them when Daddy lived here. Daddy doesn't trust frozen foods.

That afternoon when I got home from school, I went up to Jeff's hideaway. The door was closed but I heard Jeff grunting, so I knocked.

'Yeah . . .' He sounded out of breath.

'It's me, Karen.'

'Oh.'

'Can I come in?'

'Yeah . . . I guess so.'

I opened the door. Jeff was on the floor doing push-ups.

'Hey . . . your toe is unbandaged!'

'Yeah . . . Mom took me over to Dr Winters. It's fine now.'

'That's good.'

Jeff was counting. 'Eighty-five, eighty-six, eighty-seven . . .' When he got to ninety he stopped and lay flat on his stomach. He was breathing hard.

I sat down on his bed. 'Mary Louise Rumberger was over on Sunday,' I said.

'I know . . . I talked to her before.'

'She wanted to make sure you were coming to her party.'

'I know.'

'Are you?'

'Sure.'

'That's good. Jeff?'

'Yeah . . .'

'Did you have fun when you ran away?'

'I didn't run away,' he said.

'Oh. Well, was it fun when you were gone?'

'No.'

'I'm not supposed to ask any questions . . . I know that. But I just want to tell you one thing. If you went away because you wanted to stop the divorce, you better forget it. Daddy and Mom had an awful fight Friday night. They yelled and screamed and called each other a lot of names. They're just impossible together.'

'I know that, Karen.'

'Then you didn't run away to stop Daddy from flying to Las Vegas?'

'No,' Jeff said.

'But I was sure you did.'

'Well, I didn't.'

'Oh.'

'Dad was over to see me this morning.'

'He was? Was Mom home?'

'Yeah.'

'Well, what happened?'

'Nothing. She stayed upstairs the whole time.'

'Is Daddy going to Las Vegas?'

'Yeah. Tomorrow.'

'I guess I knew he would,' I said. 'Jeff . . .'

'Yeah?'

'I'm glad you came home.'

Jeff turned over and looked up at the ceiling. 'Don't ever run away, Karen. It stinks!'

'I won't. Not ever. I promise.'

Wednesday, 12 May
I will never run away. Running away does not solve
anything! Also, I will never tell anyone I went to see
Petey Mansfield yesterday. If J.N. knows, let him tell
me.

I have started to mark my days again. I am back
to C−. I just had an awful thought. Suppose there
aren't any more A+ days once you get to be twelve?
Wouldn't that be something! To spend the rest of
your life looking for an A+ day and not finding it.

Chapter 29

I got two postcards from Daddy. I wrote him back while Mrs Singer was giving us her daily lecture on manners. She told us we haven't had a real sixth-grade day all year. Now isn't that too much? Here we are getting ready for junior high and she's telling us we don't act like sixth graders yet!

Debbie says if Mrs Singer sprays hair stuff on herself once more this year she's going to report her to the principal. Imagine a teacher spraying herself in front of the class and then telling *us* we have no manners. I will be so glad to be rid of her!

This afternoon we had to fill out little green cards for next year. One question was about parents. You had to check a box telling if they were deceased or divorced. I checked *divorced*. I might as well get used to admitting it.

Tonight I found out my mother is going to sell our house! How can she do such a thing? She says she *has* to put our house up for sale. It has something to do with the divorce. I can't believe it.

I asked Mom, 'What about us? Where will we go?'

'I haven't made up my mind yet,' Mom said,

'but I'm thinking about Florida. We might as well move someplace warm as long as we're going to move.'

'Florida! That's about a million miles away,' I said. 'I'll never see Debbie again. Or Val. And what about Daddy?'

'Oh, you could see him during school vacations. It would be fun. But nothing's definite yet. So don't start worrying.'

'I'm not worrying. I just want to know what's going on.'

'Right now the only thing I can tell you for sure is that we're selling the house.'

'Daddy won't let us move to Florida,' I said. 'It's too far away.'

'It's not *that* far,' Mom said. 'You'd be able to write and phone.'

'That's not the same as seeing him!'

'Karen . . . I don't want to argue about this,' Mom said. 'I have a lot of thinking to do before I make up my mind.'

'But we *are* going to move?' I said.

'Yes . . . but I don't know where.'

'When will you know?'

'By the end of next month I hope,' Mom said.

'You mean we'll move over the summer?'

'Yes. I want everything to be set before school opens in the fall.'

'You mean I might go to a different school?'

'You probably will,' Mom said. 'Even if we wind up in an apartment around here you'll all have to change schools.'

'You mean we might take an apartment near Daddy?' I asked.

'Well, it's a possibility. Or we might take one in New York. I've always wanted to live in the city.'

'But what about your job at Global?' I said.

'It's a temporary job, Karen. I'll get a better one if we move. Or I might go to college full-time until I get my degree.'

'But what about Aunt Ruth? How could you leave her?'

'That will be good for both of us,' Mom said.

'But . . . but . . .' I couldn't think of anything else to say.

Later when I got into bed I remembered that Gary Owens said it's warm in Houston. So I went back downstairs. 'Hey, Mom . . . if we have to move, how about Houston?'

'Houston!' she said, like I was crazy or something. 'Why would we want to move there? That's in Texas.'

'I know it,' I said. 'Somebody from my class moved there. It never gets cold.'

Mom said, 'Look, Karen . . . if we move someplace warm it will be California or Florida. But Texas is out of the question. And nothing is settled yet. I told you that before.'

161

I hope my mother knows what she is doing this time. Suppose we move to Florida and then she decides she doesn't like it. Do we move back to New Jersey or do we try California or what? I have always lived right here on Woods End Road. I love our house. I don't want to move anywhere.

Chapter 30

I got my divorce book!

Debbie is very interested in divorce. Now that I have my book it will be easy to teach her all about it. Even though Debbie says her mother and father are not going to get divorced it can't hurt her to know the facts. This way she will be prepared for anything!

I talked to Val this afternoon. She says maybe my mother will meet a man when we move. I guess it could happen. Suppose she gets married and her new husband doesn't like kids? Suppose he's mean or else very old? There are too many things for me to think about.

If I do move away Val promises to keep an eye on my father and let me know if anything important comes up. I think the idea of my leaving has her feeling pretty sad. She's not looking forward to summer at all.

'I'll be around for at least another month,' I told her. 'And maybe my mother will decide to stay near here after all. We might wind up living closer than we do now.'

'Or we might not,' Val said.

'Oh, well . . . even if we don't we can still write and phone and see each other over vacations.'

'That's not the same,' Val told me.

'I know it,' I said. Poor Val. I wish there was a book to make you feel happy when you're not. I would get it for her.

I got a letter from Garfa:

Dear Karen,

I'm sorry that your mother and father are going through with their divorce. But I'm glad you're getting used to the idea. Mattie tells me not to be so upset. I'll try to accept the situation too. Don't blame yourself. You are still my most dependable Karen.

I'm going to buy the divorce book you wrote about. Maybe it will help me understand too. Your father is here and he's fine, but he misses you a lot.

Love,
Garfa

Chapter 31

Today the sixth graders were invited to spend a day at the junior high. Debbie and I went together. We toured the whole school and had our lunch in the cafeteria. There was plenty of room for us because all the ninth graders were over at the high school getting their tour. I guess Jeff feels pretty grown up now that he's almost done with junior high.

We met some of the teachers, and the principal made a short speech. He looks fairly young and sounds very nice. I wish I wasn't going to move away.

On the way home from junior high Debbie said, 'I'll really miss you this summer, Karen. I wish we weren't going away on vacation.'

'I'll miss you too,' I told her.

'You're my best friend.'

'You're mine.'

'Do you think you'll have moved by the time I get back?'

'I'm not sure. Nothing's definite yet. You know my mother.'

'Well . . . I hope Jeff doesn't forget about me,'

Debbie said. 'My mother always says, "Absence makes the heart grow fonder." '

'Mine says, "Ought of sight – out of mind." '

'Oh, Karen!' We both laughed. Debbie knew I was just teasing.

When we got to my house I said, 'Come on in . . . I want to show you my divorce book.'

'I can't,' Debbie said. 'It's Tuesday – I've got ballet.'

'That's right. How could I forget?'

'Karen . . . I've got something for you.' Debbie reached into her skirt pocket and pulled out two pictures. 'Here—' she said.

I looked at them. They were of Debbie making monkey faces.

'My father took them just for you.'

I will never find another friend like Debbie.

Jeff came out of the house then. 'Hi, Fat-and-Ugly . . . long time no see—' he said. I haven't seen Debbie smile like that in months.

We had Kentucky Fried Chicken for supper. We ate it right out of the box because Mom is taking us to the movies and we don't want to be late.

While we were eating Amy said, 'Hey, Karen, why did the man put Band-Aids in his refrigerator?' She didn't wait for me to answer. She went right on. 'Because it had cold cuts! Get it? Cold *cuts*!'

'I get it,' I said. Then I laughed. Imagine Amy telling riddles again!

I had a B+ day today.

Judy Blume talks about writing
It's Not the End of the World

When I wrote *It's Not the End of the World* in the early seventies, I lived in suburban New Jersey with my husband and two children, who were both in elementary school. I could see their concern and fear each time a family in our neighbourhood divorced. What do you say to your friends when you find out their parents are splitting up? If it could happen to them, could it happen to us?

At the time, my own marriage was in trouble, but I wasn't ready or able to admit it to myself, let alone anyone else. In the hope that it would get better, I dedicated this book to my husband. But a few years later, we, too, divorced. It was hard on all of us, more painful than I could have imagined, but somehow we muddled through, and it wasn't the end of any of our worlds, though on some days it might have felt like it.

Divorce laws have changed since I wrote this book. You don't have to go to Nevada or anyplace else to be divorced these days. And unlike Karen's mother in this book, many women have jobs outside the home, regardless of whether they're married or have children. Not that a new law or having two working parents makes divorce easy. It still hurts. It still causes the same fears and feelings Karen experiences in this story.

Are you there, God? It's me, Margaret,
again. Have you thought about it?
My growing, I mean. I've got a bra now.
It would be really nice if I had
something to put in it.

There are lots of things about growing up that
are hard to be honest about, even with your best
friends. So Margaret talks to God about her
feelings – in one of Judy Blume's funniest and
best-known novels.

Turn the page to read an extract

Chapter 1

Are you there, God? It's me, Margaret. We're moving today. I'm so scared, God. I've never lived anywhere but here. Suppose I hate my new school? Suppose everybody there hates me? Please help me, God. Don't let New Jersey be too horrible. Thank you.

We moved on the Tuesday before Labor Day. I knew what the weather was like the second I got up. I knew because I caught my mother sniffing under her arms. She always does that when it's hot and humid, to make sure her deodorant's working. I don't use deodorant yet. I don't think people start to smell bad until they're at least twelve. So I've still got a few months to go.

I was really surprised when I came home from camp and found out our New York apartment had been rented to another family and that *we* owned a house in Farbrook, New Jersey. First of all I never even heard of Farbrook. And second of all, I'm not usually left out of important family decisions.

But when I groaned, 'Why New Jersey?' I was told, 'Long Island is too social – Westchester is too expensive – and Connecticut is too inconvenient.'

So Farbrook, New Jersey it was, where my

father could commute to his job in Manhattan, where I could go to public school, and where my mother could have all the grass, trees and flowers she ever wanted. Except I never knew she wanted that stuff in the first place.

The new house is on Morningbird Lane. It isn't bad. It's part brick, part wood. The shutters and front door are painted black. Also, there is a very nice brass knocker. Every house on our new street looks a lot the same. They are all seven years old. So are the trees.

I think we left the city because of my grandmother, Sylvia Simon. I can't figure out any other reason for the move. Especially since my mother says Grandma is too much of an influence on me. It's no big secret in our family that Grandma sends me to summer camp in New Hampshire. And that she enjoys paying my private school tuition (which she won't be able to do any more because now I'll be going to public school). She even knits me sweaters that have labels sewed inside saying MADE EXPRESSLY FOR YOU . . . BY GRANDMA.

And she doesn't do all that because we're poor. I know for a fact that we're not. I mean, we aren't rich but we certainly have enough. Especially since I'm an only child. That cuts way down on food and clothes. I know this family that has seven kids and every time they go to the shoe store it costs a bundle. My mother and father didn't plan for me to be an only child, but that's the way it worked out, which is fine with me because this way I don't have anybody around to fight.

Anyhow, I figure this house-in-New-Jersey business is my parents' way of getting me away from Grandma. She doesn't have a car, she hates buses *and* she thinks all trains are dirty. So unless Grandma plans to walk, which is unlikely, I won't be seeing much of her. Now some kids might think, who cares about seeing a grandmother? But Sylvia Simon is a lot of fun, considering her age, which I happen to know is sixty. The only problem is she's always asking me if I have boyfriends and if they're Jewish. Now *that* is ridiculous because number one I don't have boyfriends. And number two what would I care if they're Jewish or not?

Chapter 2

We hadn't been in the new house more than an hour when the doorbell rang. I answered. It was this girl in a bathing suit.

'Hi,' she said. 'I'm Nancy Wheeler. The real estate agent sent out a sheet on you. So I know you're Margaret and you're in sixth grade. So am I.'

I wondered what else she knew.

'It's plenty hot, isn't it?' Nancy asked.

'Yes,' I agreed. She was taller than me and had bouncy hair. The kind I'm hoping to grow. Her nose turned up so much I could look right into her nostrils.

Nancy leaned against the door. 'Well, you want to come over and go under the sprinklers?'

'I don't know. I'll have to ask.'

'Okay. I'll wait.'

I found my mother with her rear end sticking out of a bottom kitchen cabinet. She was arranging her pots and pans.

'Hey, Mom. There's a girl here who wants to know if I can go under her sprinklers?'

'If you want to,' my mother said.

'I need my bathing suit,' I said.

'Gads, Margaret! I don't know where a bathing suit is in this mess.'

I walked back to the front door and told Nancy, 'I can't find my bathing suit.'

'You can borrow one of mine,' she said.

'Wait a second,' I said, running back to the kitchen. 'Hey, Mom. She says I can wear one of hers. Okay?'

'Okay,' my mother mumbled from inside the cabinet. Then she backed out. She spit her hair out of her face. 'What did you say her name was?'

'Umm . . . Wheeler. Nancy Wheeler.'

'Okay. Have a good time,' my mother said.

Nancy lives six houses away, also on Morning-bird Lane. Her house looks like mine but the brick is painted white and the front door and shutters are red.

'Come on in,' Nancy said.

I followed her into the foyer, then up the four stairs leading to the bedrooms. The first thing I noticed about Nancy's room was the dressing table with the heart-shaped mirror over it. Also, everything was very neat.

When I was little I wanted a dressing table like that. The kind that's wrapped up in a fluffy organdy skirt. I never got one though, because my mother likes tailored things.

Nancy opened her bottom dresser drawer. 'When's your birthday?' she asked.

'March,' I told her.

'Great! We'll be in the same class. There are

three sixth grades and they arrange us by age. I'm April.'

'Well, I don't know what class I'm in but I know it's Room Eighteen. They sent me a lot of forms to fill out last week and that was printed on all of them.'

'I told you we'd be together. I'm in Room Eighteen too.' Nancy handed me a yellow bathing suit. 'It's clean,' she said. 'My mother always washes them after a wearing.'

'Thank you,' I said, taking the suit. 'Where should I change?'

Nancy looked around the room. 'What's wrong with here?'

'Nothing,' I said. 'I don't mind if you don't mind.

'Why should I mind?'

'I don't know.' I worked the suit on from the bottom. I knew it was going to be too big. Nancy gave me the creeps the way she sat on her bed and watched me. I left my polo on until the last possible second. I wasn't about to let her see I wasn't growing yet. That was my business.

'Oh, you're still flat.' Nancy laughed.

'Not exactly,' I said, pretending to be very cool. 'I'm small boned, is all.'

'I'm growing already,' Nancy said, sticking her chest way out. 'In a few years I'm going to look like one of those girls in *Playboy*.'

Well, I didn't think so, but I didn't say anything. My father gets *Playboy* and I've seen those girls in the middle. Nancy looked like she had a long way to go. Almost as far as me.

'Want me to do up your straps?' she asked.

'Okay.'

'I figured you'd be real grown up coming from New York. City girls are supposed to grow up a lot faster. Did you ever kiss a boy?'

'You mean really kiss? On the lips?' I asked.

'Yes,' Nancy said impatiently. 'Did you?'

'Not really,' I admitted.

Nancy breathed a sigh of relief. 'Neither did I.'

I was overjoyed. Before she said that I was beginning to feel like some kind of underdeveloped little kid.

'I practise a lot though,' Nancy said.

'Practise what?' I asked.

'Kissing! Isn't that what we were talking about? *Kissing!*'

'How can you practise that?' I asked.

'Watch this.' Nancy grabbed her bed pillow and embraced it. She gave it a long kiss. When she was done she threw the pillow back on the bed. 'It's important to experiment, so when the time comes you're all ready. I'm going to be a great kisser some day. Want to see something else?'

I just stood there with my mouth half open.

Nancy sat down at her dressing table and opened a drawer. 'Look at this,' she said.

I looked. There were a million little bottles, jars and tubes. There were more cosmetics in that drawer than my mother had all together. I asked, 'What do you do with all that stuff?'

'It's another one of my experiments. To see how I look best. So when the times comes I'll be ready.' She opened a lipstick and painted on a bright pink mouth. 'Well, what do you think?'

'Umm . . . I don't know. It's kind of bright, isn't it?'

Nancy studied herself in the heart-shaped mirror. She rubbed her lips together. 'Well, maybe you're right.' She wiped off the lipstick with a tissue. 'My mother would kill me if I came out like this anyway. I can't wait till eighth grade. That's when I'll be allowed to wear lipstick every day.'

Then she whipped out a hairbrush and started to brush her long, brown hair. She parted it in the middle and caught it at the back with a barrette. 'Do you always wear your hair like that?' she asked me.

My hand went up to the back of my neck. I felt all the bobby pins I'd used to pin my hair up so my neck wouldn't sweat. I knew it looked terrible. 'I'm letting it grow,' I said. 'It's at that in-between stage now. My mother thinks I should wear it over my ears though. My ears stick out a little.'

'I noticed,' Nancy said.

I got the feeling that Nancy noticed *everything*!

'Ready to go?' she asked.

'Sure.'

She opened a linen closet in the hall and handed me a purple towel. I followed her down the stairs and into the kitchen, where she grabbed two peaches out of the refrigerator and handed one to me. 'Want to meet my mom?' she asked.

'Okay,' I said, taking a bite of my peach.

'She's thirty-eight, but tells us she's twenty-five. Isn't that a scream!' Nancy snorted.

Mrs Wheeler was on the porch with her legs tucked under her and a book on her lap. I couldn't tell what book it was. She was suntanned and had the same nose as Nancy.

'Mom, this is Margaret Simon who just moved in down the street.'

Mrs Wheeler took off her glasses and smiled at me.

'Hello,' I said.

'Hello, Margaret. I'm very glad to meet you. You're from New York, aren't you?'

'Yes, I am.'

'East side or West?'

'We lived on West Sixty-seventh. Near Lincoln Center.'

'How nice. Does your father still work in the city?'

'Yes.'

'And what does he do?'

'He's in insurance.' I sounded like a computer.

'How nice. Please tell your mother I'm looking forward to meeting her. We've got a Morningbird Lane bowling team on Mondays and a bridge game every Thursday afternoon and a . . .'

'Oh, I don't think my mother knows how to bowl and she wouldn't be interested in bridge. She paints most of the day,' I explained.

'She paints?' Mrs Wheeler asked.

'Yes.'

'How interesting. What does she paint?'

'Mostly pictures of fruits and vegetables. Sometimes flowers too.'

Mrs Wheeler laughed. 'Oh, you mean *pictures*! I thought you meant walls! Tell your mother we're making our car pools early this year. We'd be happy to help her arrange hers . . . especially Sunday school. That's always the biggest problem.'

'I don't go to Sunday school.'

'You don't?'

'No.'

'*Lucky!*' Nancy shouted.

'Nancy, *please*!' Mrs Wheeler said.

'Hey, Mom . . . Margaret came to go under the

11

sprinkler with me, not to go through the third degree.'

'All right. If you see Evan tell him I want to talk to him.'

Nancy grabbed me by the hand and pulled me outside. 'I'm sorry my mother's so nosey.'

'I didn't mind,' I said. 'Who's Evan?'

'He's my brother. He's disgusting!'

'Disgusting how?' I asked.

'Because he's fourteen. All boys of fourteen are disgusting. They're only interested in two things – pictures of naked girls and dirty books!'

Nancy really seemed to know a lot. Since I didn't know any boys of fourteen I took her word for it.

Nancy turned on the outside tap and adjusted it so that the water sprayed lightly from the sprinkler. 'Follow the leader!' she called, running through the water. I guessed Nancy was the leader.

She jumped through the spray. I followed. She turned cartwheels. I tried but didn't make it. She did leaps through the air. I did too. She stood straight under the spray. I did the same. That's when the water came on full blast. We both got drenched, including our hair.

'Evan, you stinker!' Nancy shrieked. 'I'm telling!' She ran off to the house and left me alone with two boys.

'Who're you?' Evan asked.

'I'm Margaret. We just moved in.'

'Oh. This is Moose,' he said, pointing to the other boy.

I nodded.

'Hey,' Moose said. 'If you just moved in, ask your father if he's interested in having me cut his lawn. Five bucks a week and I trim too. What'd you say your last name was?'

'I didn't. But it's Simon.' I couldn't help thinking about what Nancy said – that all they were interested in was dirty books and naked girls. I held my towel tight around me in case they were trying to sneak a look down my bathing suit.

'*Evan! Come in here this instant!*' Mrs Wheeler hollered from the porch.

'I'm coming . . . I'm coming,' Evan muttered.

After Evan went inside Moose said, 'Don't forget to tell your father. *Moose Freed.* I'm in the phone book.'

'I won't forget,' I promised.

Moose nibbled a piece of grass. Then the back door slammed and Nancy came out, red-eyed and sniffling.

'Hey, Nancy baby! Can't you take a joke?' Moose asked.

'Shut up, animal!' Nancy yelled. Then she turned to me. 'I'm sorry they had to act like that on your first day here. Come on, I'll walk you home.'

Nancy had my clothes wrapped up in a little bundle. She was still in her wet suit. She pointed out who lived in each house between mine and hers.

'We're going to the beach for Labor Day weekend,' she said. 'So call for me on the first day of school and we'll walk together. I'm absolutely dying to know who our teacher's going to be. Miss Phipps, who we were supposed to have, ran off with some guy to California last June. So we're getting somebody new.'

When we got to my house I told Nancy if she'd wait a minute I'd give her back her bathing suit.

'I don't need it in a hurry. Tell your mother to wash it and you can give it back next week. It's an old one.'

I was sorry she told me that. Even if I'd already guessed it. I mean, probably I wouldn't lend a stranger my best bathing suit either. But I wouldn't come right out and say it.

'Oh, listen, Margaret,' Nancy said. 'On the first day of school wear loafers, but no socks.'

'How come?'

'Otherwise you'll look like a baby.'

'Oh.'

'Besides, I want you to join my secret club and if you're wearing socks the other kids might not want you.'

'What kind of secret club?' I asked.

14

'I'll tell you about it when school starts.'

'Okay,' I said.

'And remember – no socks!'

'I'll remember.'

We went to a hamburger place for supper. I told my father about Moose Freed. 'Only five bucks a cutting and he trims too.'

'No, thanks,' my father said. 'I'm looking forward to cutting it myself. That's one of the reasons we moved out here. Gardening is good for the soul.' My mother beamed. They were really driving me crazy with all that good-for-the-soul business. I wondered when they became such nature lovers!

Later, when I was getting ready for bed, I walked into a closet, thinking it was the bathroom. Would I ever get used to living in this house? When I finally made it into bed and turned out the light, I saw shadows on my wall. I tried to shut my eyes and not think about them but I kept checking to see if they were still there. I couldn't fall asleep.

Are you there, God? It's me, Margaret. I'm in my new bedroom but I still have the same bed. It's so quiet here at night – nothing like the city. I see shadows on my wall and hear these funny creaking sounds. It's scary, God! Even though my father says all houses make noises and the shadows are only trees. I hope he knows what

15

he's talking about! I met a girl today. Her name's Nancy. She expected me to be very grown up. I think she was disappointed. Don't you think it's time for me to start growing, God? If you could arrange it I'd be very glad. Thank you.

My parents don't know I actually talk to God. I mean, if I told them they'd think I was some kind of religious fanatic or something. So I keep it very private. I can talk to him without moving my lips if I have to. My mother says God is a nice idea. He belongs to everybody.